Praise for *Innocence; or, Murder on Steep Street*

An NPR Best Book of the Year

"The great draw of *Innocence; or, Murder on Steep Street* is the menacing view it gives us of communist Prague . . . Kovály channels Chandler but takes him into a landscape far, far away from wide-open LA."—Maureen Corrigan, NPR's *Fresh Air*

"An extraordinary novel . . . A remarkable work of art with the intrigue of a spy puzzle, the irony of a political fable, the shrewdness of a novel of manners, and the toughness of a hard-boiled murder mystery."   —Tom Nolan, *The Wall Street Journal*

"A luminous testament from a dark time, *Innocence* is at once a clever *hommage* to Raymond Chandler, and a portrait of a city—Prague—caught and held fast in a state of Kafkaesque paranoia. Only a great survivor could have written such a book."   —John Banville

"The plot is easy to envision as film noir . . . As for innocence, the woman who went to hell twice wants her readers to know that there is no such thing."—*The Times Literary Supplement*

"Purely Chandleresque."   —*Toronto Star*

"Kovály's prose carries echoes of Albert Camus' novels . . . Yet, *Innocence* is astonishingly—and brilliantly—written as a thriller in the style of Raymond Chandler, an author Kovály hugely admired. The mean streets her characters tread are infinitely more treacherous than the dark blocks of Los Angeles but she creates a plot packed with surprise, a character-driven, murderous matrix that sustains an amoral universe in an all-too-convincing story."   —*The Jewish Chronicle*

INNOCENCE

OR, MURDER ON STEEP STREET

HEDA

MARGOLIUS

KOVÁLY

TRANSLATED FROM THE CZECH
BY ALEX ZUCKER

First published in Czech as *Nevina aneb Vražda v Příkré ulici* in 1985 by Index, Köln, Germany.
Second Czech edition published in 2013 by Mladá fronta, Praha, Czech Republic.

Published by
Soho Press, Inc.
853 Broadway
New York, NY 10003

Library of Congress Cataloging-in-Publication Data

Kovály, Heda, 1919–2010.
[Nevina. English]
Innocence; or, Murder on Steep Street / Heda Margolius Kovály; translated by Alex Zucker.
"First published in Czech as Nevina in 1985 by Index, Köln, Germany. Second edition in Czech
published in 2013 by Mladá fronta, Praha"
1. Motion picture theaters—Fiction. 2. Murder—Investigation—Fiction. 3. Czechoslovakia—
Fiction. I. Zucker, Alex, translator. II. Title. III. Title: Murder on Steep Street.

PG5039.21.O8485N4813 2015
891.8'6354—dc23 2014042467

ISBN 978-1-61695-645-5
eISBN 978-1-61695-497-0

Interior design by Janine Agro, Soho Press, Inc.

Printed in the United States of America

10 9 8 7 6 5 4 3 2 1

INNOCENCE

INTRODUCTION

Ivan Margolius, son of Heda Margolius Kovály

IN THE MID-1960S, the Czechoslovak political situation was becoming less traumatic: when the Communist regime started to loosen its grip, foreign travel was being gradually allowed and everyday produce became more available. We were living in our new apartment in Strašnice. It was on the second floor of a building constructed using the typical concrete panels so ubiquitous in the suburbs circling Prague's famous historical center. We had managed to wangle these living quarters following the official court annulment of the verdict against my father and as compensation for our inner-city flat, which had been confiscated by the Communist authorities after my father's judicial murder in 1952. Heda was working on a translation of "The King in Yellow," a story by Raymond Chandler, first published in 1938. As I studied for my university exams in the bedroom, she worked in our living room, first writing the translation out long-hand with a blue ballpoint pen in lined notebooks, then typing up a clean copy. Now and then she'd ask for advice, shouting through the walls: "What word would you use for 'a big, tall man' if you were talking with your friends?" After a few moments I'd respond: *"Habán?"* "That's what I thought," she'd shout back cheerfully.

My mother, Heda Bloch (1919–2010), was born into a Jewish family in Prague. Her life was carefree until the Third Reich occupation of Sudetenland in October 1938, which led to the takeover of the rest of Czechoslovakia in March 1939. Two years later, she and her first husband, my father, Rudolf Margolius, together with her parents, were transported to the Łódź (Litzmannstadt) ghetto in occupied Poland.

In August 1944, on the ghetto liquidation, they were all transferred to Auschwitz, where Heda lost her parents, who were led away to the gas chambers on arrival. Heda was also separated from Rudolf, who after several weeks in Auschwitz was relocated to Kaufbeuren and Mühldorf in Germany, digging trenches and working on construction of secret underground aircraft hangars. He eventually ended up in Dachau. Heda likewise was moved to labor camps in the Gross Rosen area. When the eastern front was approaching in February 1945, the women prisoners were organized into a death march from what is now Poland to the Bergen-Belsen camp in Germany. Heda escaped from the march and managed to reach Prague, where she hid, with the assistance of the Czech partisans, till the end of the war.

In the early days of May 1945, in the time of the Prague Uprising, Heda helped by carrying ammunition during the fighting for the liberation of the city. Rudolf had survived Dachau, escaping the march out of the camp. On encountering the US Army he acted as an interpreter and leader of the Garmisch-Partenkirchen survivors' collection camp. In June 1945, Rudolf and Heda were reunited in Prague.

With optimism and hope for a better and just society, Heda and Rudolf Margolius began their post-war life in Prague. Rudolf became a member of the Communist Party. During the war his parents had been shot following their transport to Riga. He had endured humiliation and suffering in the Nazi labor and concentration camps and was impressed by how the Communists helped other detainees there. He had resolved to help create a prosperous welfare state without social class divisions and racial prejudice. Heda perceived, though, that the new politicians gaining power were corrupt and dishonest with their extreme behavior and drastic policies. However, Rudolf, full of determination, managed to persuade her of his point of view. With reluctance, Heda joined the Party too.

After the Communist takeover of Czechoslovakia in 1948, Rudolf became deputy minister of foreign trade, in charge of economic agreements with the capitalist countries. Over the next four years, despite the efforts of many experts and partly due to the enforced exports of Czechoslovak goods, foodstuffs, and mineral resources to the Soviet Union, the centralized economy began to fail, and the Czechoslovak Communist Party and its Soviet advisers sought scapegoats.

Heda feared for Rudolf's safety and tried to make him leave his post, but he insisted that he was ordered by the Party to carry on in his duties as there was no one to replace him. In January 1952 he was arrested following the detention of the Communist deputy leader, Slánský. Accused unjustly of "anti-state conspiracy" and sentenced in a show trial, Rudolf was executed in December 1952.

The Slánský Trial, in which eleven out of fourteen innocent defendants were sentenced to death for the fabricated offenses of spying and sabotage, became one of the most significant episodes of the Communist rule on the European continent in the 1950s. Its outcome affected not only the fate of our family, but lives of thousands of other Czechoslovak citizens and even peoples of the neighboring countries. The trial's purpose, after Yugoslavia's defection in 1948, was to deter any deviation from the Soviet camp. The Soviet Union's paranoia about the vulnerability of its borders and its security, which persists to this day, had to be satisfied by a solid protective zone of loyal Communist countries.

Heda survived because of her determination to fight back despite all the obstacles placed in front of her: if Hitler had not managed to destroy her, then the Soviets and the Communists would not do so either. As a persecuted wife of a "traitor" and a political undesirable, she had managed to look after us both, scraping a living by designing book dust jackets and weaving carpets.

In 1955 she married her second husband, Pavel Kovály, who suggested, because of Heda's knowledge and love of languages, that she should try her hand at translation. She translated into Czech the books of well-known German, British, and American authors and passed them on to publishers, initially using Pavel's name to submit her work, as she herself was not allowed to earn a living.

In August 1968 Warsaw Pact countries invaded Czechoslovakia and Heda fled the country. By then I was living in London, having left Prague in 1966. As soon as I had discovered all the details of Rudolf's fate I decided I could no longer trust, and live in, the country of my birth and sought refuge in Britain, the oldest democracy. By then Pavel was lecturing in Boston, Massachusetts. Heda joined Pavel and subsequently worked at the Harvard Law School Library beginning in the fall of 1975.

She wrote her memoir, *Under a Cruel Star,* first published in 1973, soon after coming to the United States, on my insistence; I demanded to know her story and knew the world audience would also benefit. The book was so well received and respected that Clive James included a chapter about Heda in his book *Cultural Amnesia* (2007), a survey of significant personalities of the 20th century.

Heda translated many authors, including Arnold Zweig, Heinrich Böll, H. G. Wells, Arnold Bennett, Arthur Miller, Edna Ferber, Budd Schulberg, Irwin Shaw, John Steinbeck, Philip Roth, Saul Bellow, William Golding, Muriel Spark and Kingsley Amis. But perhaps the author she admired most was Raymond Chandler. She rendered into the Czech three of his novels, *Farewell, My Lovely*; *The High Window;* and

The Little Sister, and her translations are still being printed by Prague publishing houses to this day, fifty years later. It was Chandler's style of writing she liked so much: his depiction of characters and their way of speaking, as well as his scenic descriptions and strong sense of place. That inspiration led her to start working on crime fiction of her own, based on a period she had lived through herself. She used her own painful and extraordinary experience and, with this non-traditional crime fiction approach, tackled a subject that is hardly ever treated in the Czech or world literature.

She began writing the story in the early 1980s, and being rather modest, decided to bring it out under pseudonym of Helena Nováková (Helena was Heda's middle name), the same name as one of the main heroines of the story. *Nevina* (*Innocence*) was first published in 1985 by Index, a Czech émigré press based in Köln, Germany. This was in the post-invasion time of so-called "normalization," a return to stricter living conditions in Czechoslovakia, and she did not want to create any difficulties for her friends living in Prague. That is the reason for the book's initial obscurity. On return to Prague in 1996, Heda corrected the original book publication, penning her name on the title page as the real author. However, the book remained on her library shelves and only after her passing was *Nevina* republished in Prague, bearing her rightful name, in 2013.

Innocence is set in Prague in the 1950s, at a historical moment of extreme political oppression. Since the bloodless coup in February 1948—when the Czechoslovak Communist Party and its leader, Klement Gottwald, replaced the government, which had been led by the pre-war democratic parties and President Edvard Beneš, successor to Tomáš Masaryk—the majority of Czechoslovak population had been living in fear.

In the late 1940s and 1950s the political atmosphere was highly charged in Communist Czechoslovakia. The Communists introduced censorship, restricted foreign travel, and purged the Ministry of Interior's democratically placed personnel, installing their own people in key positions even prior to the coup. State Security, encouraged and coached by secretly imported Soviet advisers, began to use Soviet-inspired methods to suppress personal freedom and reinforce one-party ideology and alliance to the Soviet Union. Many citizens used to the democratic regime the country had enjoyed during the prosperous period between the wars had to reorient their public face to conform to the Soviet-inspired policies and restrictions.

In this climate of growing economic and political

difficulties, suitable scapegoats were sought to keep discontent in check. More than two hundred fifty thousand citizens were arrested and imprisoned for allegedly working against the Party and terror gripped the country. Public show trials and secret military tribunals were staged; a large number of people accused of spying and sabotage were sentenced to death, hard labor, or long-term imprisonment. Corrupt Party officials used this perverted approach to retain power, instigating verdicts of guilt of sabotage or espionage when a colleague's removal was to their advantage. Accused loyal Communists accepted their charges without a fight, believing falsely that by doing so they would further the good cause of the regime. Citizens tried to emulate their leaders' bad behavior in order to survive. People had to adopt a double life, a public one in which they supported the Communist regime, and a private one, rigorously guarded, where they expressed their true opinions and misgivings only to close relatives and friends. Even then they had to be careful because some family members reported on one another to the State Security, either out of desperation or to improve their economic or social status. Society and community structure, friendships, marriages, family links, and employment relationships suffered as a consequence, reshaping the whole character of the nation.

Heda's novel, *Innocence*, was inspired by Chandler's Philip Marlowe, who seeks out the guilty amongst the innocents within the corrupt and decadent American dream society. In a way, Marlowe's struggles are similar to Helena Nováková's efforts to make her existence worthwhile in an environment devoid of respect for human life. The innocence theme of the book came from Hemingway's quote in *A Moveable Feast,* according to which all real evil starts from innocence. Several personalities in the book see acts like lying, misrepresenting, informing, and betraying confidences as inconsequential, trivial matters, thus diluting the difference between guilt and innocence. Even murder is perceived as an accident for which no one is to blame.

In the intensely complex psychological drama, the heroine, Helena Nováková, is an almost-autobiographical portrait of Heda during her most trying times, when her first husband was arrested and then murdered in a political show trial. She depicts how she felt and thought, how the ordinary people around her behaved, how they tried to overcome the stranglehold of the Communist regime. Similar to the characters in Albert Camus's fictional universes, all of Heda's characters are guilty to various degrees, although they all declaim their innocence.

Heda uses Helena's friend Šípek's words to describe subtly in Orwellian theme how Communist Czechoslovakia treated its peoples and justified its actions: "Experts agree that animals are almost like people . . . as long as they've got a nice place to live and something to keep them entertained, they can do without freedom . . . In a good zoo, where they're well-fed and have a chance to socialize, most animals are happier than they would be . . . in lonely and dangerous freedom."

In Helena, Heda expresses private notions, fears, and attitudes she could not have written in such detail in her memoir. The novel *Innocence* allowed her to reveal much more of her inner mind and feelings, her views on life and morals in a fractured incarcerated society. It is a true companion to her memoir.

Bedford, September 2014

All things truly wicked start from an innocence.
—Ernest Hemingway, *A Moveable Feast*

The world is a sphere, slightly flattened at the poles, spinning inside my head. Everything on it is clearly marked: the mossy forest trail, the dewdrops on a spiderweb suspended between branches, the pebbles under water as translucent as liquid light, the African shanty overgrown with lilacs. There is the snow-peaked mountain, crisscrossed with skiers' tracks; there are the bridges and the rivers and the millions of little white paws racing ashore with the tide to pause an instant at our feet. The faces long since faded, and the voices that have died away, and the iridescent white outlines of ideas. And trickling into the oceans, to keep them from drying up, every now and then a drop of blood.

Sometimes I have to erase something and redraw it, but I'm not very good, so the original always shows through. The old colors are durable. But it doesn't matter if people can see the corrections, that's all right, because my world is complete, painstakingly crafted: my world, a sphere, slightly flattened at the poles, spinning inside my head.

PART I

1

I GOT OFF the tram at Můstek and walked the rest
of the way. It was a windy day in early spring, the
kind when a person ought to be out in a field or in
the woods, and every moment not spent boxed-up
indoors is precious. Even though I was in a rush, I
took the time to stop and look at a couple of shop
windows.

So what? No use driving myself crazy over another
minute or two. I was in for a tough shift today anyway.
Me, always so careful to stay out of conflict and keep
to myself. Of all people, why did the boss have to go
and pick me?

A curtain of shadow dropped behind me as I stepped into the cinema lobby. I swiveled my head to look at the display case for Fotografia, the state-run photography studio. A bride in a veil holding a bouquet. The same one for six months now. When they first put her up she looked beautiful. Now her blissful smile had turned as sour as yesterday's milk. A moment in time, snared in a lasso, strangled as it tried to escape. To the left, set in a long blank wall, was the gray-painted metal door that led to the projection booth. I stopped a moment, hesitating.

Janeček, poor guy, was in for a tongue-lashing from the boss, and maybe the head office too. Twenty-eight and single, with six years' experience as a projectionist, he had turned up four months ago with a recommendation from the job placement office. Didn't talk to a soul. None of the ushers had managed to break him. Those girls tried every trick in the book. Especially Marie. She was eating her heart out having an unmarried man within reach who wouldn't climb in the sack with her. Janeček was a good worker, too, punctual and polite. God only knows what got into him yesterday. Must have mixed up the reels or something. The movie started halfway through, in the middle of a chase scene: cars speeding around the curve, tires squealing, faces flashing past. At first the audience figured it for an unusually creative opening sequence, but then the whistling started. The boss was out of town at a conference for three days. She called after the screening to see if everything went all right, and when Marie told her about the slipup, the boss asked to talk to me.

"Listen, Helena, tomorrow's my last day of meetings. You're the only one there with any brains. Will you talk to Janeček for me? He won't take it so hard coming from you. Try to be tactful, but make sure you get the message across. Either he does his job right or I find a replacement. There's plenty of projectionists out there, and good ones too. You think he drinks? Take a look around the booth, if you don't mind. I'm sure if he's got any bottles up there, he'll clear them out before I get back. All right, thanks for handling this. I'll give you a call back tomorrow."

As soon as someone flatters you for your brains, you know trouble's coming. Marie could get through to Janeček much better and quicker than I ever could. What did brains have to do with it? But the manager had asked me, and when the boss told us to do something, we jumped. It never even crossed my mind to tell her no.

The manager was so self-assured she didn't even hide the fact that she was over forty. Though she easily could have. She was still a knockout, and the way she dressed, when she crossed the street, every eye was glued to her, as tubby Ládinka, our homeliest usher, said with a sigh every time. The boss's husband was a famous surgeon, and the looks he gave her after twenty years of marriage were the kind most gals only get about two months before their wedding and three months afterward. She didn't work for the money, of course. She did it because she felt like it, so every door was open to her and people fell all over themselves to get in her good graces. Everything she did was like some precious gift to the world; for her, the cinema wasn't the daily grind it was for the rest of us working stiffs, for whom the job was just a way to earn a living. But in spite of the gap between us, in spite of the boss's imported dresses and the big shiny car waiting for her out in front of the cinema every night, most of us didn't envy her. Somehow she gave the impression it was all in the natural order of things. People tend to think of happiness like a cake: if one person gets a bigger slice, it means less for everyone else. But our boss seemed to be one of those creatures that can only exist in a state of happiness and prosperity, like a deep-sea fish that can only survive at the bottom of the ocean and anywhere else it would die.

If it was true, as I'd always believed, that life was like a game of bridge—to win, you needed to know the rules and how to play the game, but you also had to be dealt a decent hand—then the boss got all the trumps. But besides that, or maybe in spite of it, she was a wise woman, and fair, and all of us ushers were grateful for that, so we bent over backwards to do what she asked. Which was why right now I was obediently trotting down the hall to that ugly gray door, even though it was the last thing on earth I wanted to do.

If only Janeček weren't such an oddball. The only person he was on friendly terms with was Josef, Marie's eight-year-old nephew, her sister Žofie's son. Žofie worked shifts in a factory, so Josef came to see Marie practically every day. And of course for a boy like him a film projector was the greatest thing since sliced bread. It was just "Hi, Marie," and whoosh, off he went, up the stairs to the booth. It was good for the kid. At least he wasn't just loafing around, and he might even learn something useful. The two of them got on surprisingly well. Janeček never talked down to him either, always spoke to him man to man. He must've been a good person, at heart, to like kids like that.

Well, here we go.

I opened the door without knocking to find Janeček standing there, leaning against the wall. I hoped he wasn't drunk. *Better get this over with quick.*

"Hello, Mr. Janeček. The boss called to say the conference won't wrap up till tomorrow. She heard what happened yesterday and wanted to know if you could explain."

Janeček didn't even blink, just stared at a dusty table littered with a half-eaten roll, a dirty rag, a big pair of scissors for cutting film, some empty movie reels, and assorted other junk. *Strange little cubbyhole*, I thought uneasily. *I'd go off my rocker in here after a week.* Murky light, rickety floorboards, dirt on every surface. Janeček acted like he didn't even notice. *Must have a pretty good hangover. He looks like death warmed over. Jesus, I've got to get out of here, this guy gives me the creeps. Did he even hear what I said? Why isn't he answering? Maybe he's too upset.*

"Try not to take it too hard, Mr. Janeček. These things happen. Just let me know what to tell the boss when she calls back."

Janeček kept his lip buttoned.

"After all, it's not a catastrophe, right? I mean sure, you made a mistake, but it can happen to anyone. It's not a matter of life and death." I forced a laugh. What was I babbling?

Janeček gazed blankly past me at the wall. Finally he dropped his eyes back to the cluttered tabletop and snapped: "You tell the boss this. Tell her anyone can make a mistake. We wouldn't want anything worse to happen. And tell her I can guarantee it'll never happen again. You make sure you tell her that. Tell her it'll never happen again, I guarantee."

"Well, all right. In any case I'm sure she'll want to speak with you when she gets back. Just be careful from now on. And forget about it, you know? It's not as if someone got shot."

Thank God I'm out of there, I thought as I left Janeček in the projection room.

I nodded to the box-office girl and unhooked the rope barring access to the stairs. I walked downstairs and turned down the hall toward the staff cloakroom to change into my uniform. Even before I reached the door, I could already hear the voices inside, cackling and chattering over each other like barnyard hens.

Good lord, at it again with the nasty gossip. Another one of those days.

I opened the door. Marie stood in the middle of the tiny room, her eyes red, with bags underneath so big you could put groceries in them. She was sobbing at the top of her lungs, a man's handkerchief bunched in her hand. Whenever she had a serious cold, or a serious heartache, she used a handkerchief left behind

by one of her ex-lovers. The other ushers stood in a
circle around her, mouths agape.

"For God's sake, girls, what's going on in here?" I
said. "It's half past two, you should be out on the floor,
we'll be opening the doors soon."

"You're not gonna believe it," Líba said. "Marie's
nephew is missing!" The whole commotion started
back up again.

"Will all of you just shut up for a minute? Now tell
me, Marie, what happened?"

"Well," Marie whimpered, "Žofie had a shift yesterday afternoon, so her boy Josef said he was comin'
over here. Sometimes I don't feel like draggin' him
all the way over the bridge to Žofie's and makin' the
trip back home again, so he just brings his schoolbag
with him, sleeps over at my place, and goes straight
to school in the morning. So when yesterday he was a
no-show, I just figured he went to stay at the Musils',
since he's friends with their son, little Petr, from school,
and his mom works at the factory too, so when she's
home sometimes she takes the boys, and when Žofie's
got the morning shift Petr comes over to her place. So,
like I said, I figured Josef was at the Musils' and Žofie
figured he was with me."

"So but this morning . . ." tubby Ládinka jumped
in. Of all the girls she had the lowest tolerance for

awkward moments of silence. "This morning Žofie calls Marie here—"

"—and she says, Hi, Marie, thanks for takin' my boy last night. You know if he got his math homework done? And I say, What're you talkin' about? Josef never came over, I thought he was with the Musils. And she says, Jesus, are you serious? Anna's got a sore throat and dropped Petr off at her sister's, so where could my boy be? She goes tearin' over to school and no sign of him there. She already called the police. Nobody's seen the kid since yesterday afternoon. Last one to lay eyes on him was Vejvodová, in the food mart 'cross the street. She says he stopped in around half past one for an ice cream bar, and his schoolbag's still at home."

"That isn't entirely correct, Miss Vránová," said a voice, and everyone turned to see a powerfully built, tan-faced man in a dark suit with a silver crew cut standing in the door. His eyes, round and bright, stood out against his dark skin like the opening in the lens of an old-fashioned camera. He wasn't tall, but his frame filled the doorway.

He took a step inside. "I'm Captain Nedoma," he said, pausing before he went on. "Miss Šulcová saw the Vrba boy in here yesterday afternoon, just before two. Right upstairs here, at the snack bar. He bought another ice cream."

The silence was so complete you could hear everyone breathe.

Then tubby Ládinka stammered: "But, but, the box office girl doesn't even come in till two. The only one here before then is . . ."

"That's right, normally there's only one person here before two P.M. We've informed your manager. They're driving her over from headquarters right now. The Horizon will be closed for today, but don't anyone go anywhere. You can have a seat in the smoking lounge. Comrade Dolejš here will wait with you. Miss Vránová, you stay here."

He jerked his head into the hallway and a blond beanpole of a man emerged from behind him with a badly healed broken nose and a suspicious bulge in his jacket.

We marched single file out of the staff cloakroom and—right face, hut!—turned into the smoking lounge. The beanpole settled in on a hard chair in the corner, looking as if he planned to spend the rest of his life there.

All of us lit up as if on command, even the girls who didn't normally smoke. The folds under tubby Ládinka's chin started trembling. Mrs. Kouřimská turned her back to the officer, crossed herself, folded her hands in her lap, and shut her eyes.

Marie, our resident authority on matters of love, had this to say about Mrs. Kouřimská: "She's livin' proof of how stupid guys are. Look at her: not a lick of makeup, sweaters faded and washed out, skirts worn through at the seat, and still looks like she just stepped off a pedestal at that whatchamacallit in Paris, the Loover. Ever since she got widowed, though, she's been all on her own. Just sits out in the park on Žofín every night in summer, watchin' the young lovers neck out the corner of her eye."

It was true. Even at fifty Mrs. Kouřimská radiated the kind of eternal beauty you don't see too much in this world, so it tends to scare people off. It was unfamiliar, almost mysterious. None of us would ever have dreamed of calling her "Karla." We treated her with respect, and called her "missus," the same as the customers.

Sitting in the smoking lounge at the Horizon with the door shut, you couldn't hear anything from the next room over, let alone from upstairs. We thought it was impossible, but we perked up our ears all the same, sitting on the edge of our seats. It felt like something might happen at any moment—maybe Josef would come bursting in, laughing about how scared we all looked and, boy, did he put one over on us, or suddenly there might be a scream or a gunshot. When you're that wound up, you always expect some kind of loud noise, something to match your inner tension, to balance it out and calm you down so the earth can settle back into its regular rotation.

But the only thing that happened was the manager walked in, pale and on the verge of fainting, followed by the man with the silver crew cut. They said we could all go home now. And that was that.

There wasn't a trace of Marie in the cloakroom, and a bunch of cops in uniform stood at the top of the stairs. The door to Janeček's cubbyhole was propped open, and inside, two handyman types in plainclothes were bent over the floor. Next to them sat a stack of pried-up floorboards, the same ones I'd felt wobble under my feet a few hours earlier.

The next day it was all over the papers:

> *Twenty-eight-year old Jiří Janeček, previously convicted for sexual offenses, lured eight-year-old Josef Vrba into the projection booth at the Horizon Cinema and attempted to sexually assault him. When the boy resisted, the suspect stabbed him to death with a pair of scissors for splicing film and hid the body under the floor. The suspect, who was just released from prison five months ago, did not resist arrest. The boy's mother had a nervous*

breakdown and is currently receiving treatment in
the hospital.

Our manager may not have had a breakdown herself, but
she sure came close. She called me into her office and
brewed me a cup of coffee with her very own two hands.

"My God, Helena, forgive me! I sent you in there
with that insane killer and the whole time he had a
dead child under the floor and heaven knows what
was going through that head of his when you—he
could've . . . Lord have mercy! And poor little Josef,
such a nice boy, always so cheerful . . ."

We sat together a good long while, crying into our
coffee.

Twenty-nine years ago, by some terrible accident,
two cells that should never have met joined to create
something that should never have existed—a little
slip of nature, happens all the time. And as those cells
divided and grew and multiplied, that little discrepancy
crystallized inside them. Maybe it was something you
could see. Maybe a little black dot, the size of the head
of a pin, and if I were a brain surgeon I could point to
it with the tip of my scalpel and say to my assistant:
"There, you see? That tiny spot on the cortex? That's
the death of Josef Vrba, age eight, of Prague." So you
see, we can't blame Mr. Janeček. He wasn't any more

responsible than the pair of scissors he used to commit the awful crime. The whole thing was caused by that little dot on his brain.

I went home. Home at this point was a studio flat I had received in a swap with the Součeks. They took our two-room flat and threw in a few thousand extra, which kept me afloat the first few weeks, till I landed myself a job.

All in all, I made out all right. I had a decent place, a job that paid. Not much, but I got by. I might have been hard up, but Karel was even worse off—not to mention Žofie. I couldn't complain. There's so much suffering in the world and everyone's suffering looks different, but it's always the same story in the end: life just glides along, until all of a sudden one day everything goes off the rails.

Karel worked in the Department of Economic Planning. We'd only been hitched two years, and loved each other madly. I mean we still did now, but it was so good for us back then, maybe too good. We were deaf and blind to everything wrong around us. Like a pair of those spiders that carry air down underwater from the surface, bubble by bubble, and attach it to a plant or a rock. Then when the bubble gets big enough, they just move inside it and live there, all nice and cozy, and the air and the water, the two elements, combine to form a wall that reflects the inside like a mirror and they can't see out of it.

Karel had a secretary—nice gal, a bit on the shy side. One Monday morning the previous September, she walked in with a letter for him to sign that had five mistakes. "Jana, dear, is there something wrong?" Karel asked. Then he looked at her and saw that she was glowing all over. Like a little bowlegged ball of sunshine standing there in front of him.

"I'm sorry," Jana said. "I'll do it over. My mind just isn't on work today."

"What is it?" Karel asked.

"Well, I guess I can tell you," she said. "My boy-friend just flew in from out of town."

"Why, that's great," Karel said. "You kids enjoy your-selves."

That night we were at home watching TV—we used to love just sitting around like that, the two of us—and Karel said to me: "Jana always was such a mousy little thing. You know, it almost made me feel sorry for her. Forget the damn dictation. I'm just glad to see she's actually got some woman in her."

If only I'd kept my trap shut, but no: "Why don't you invite her and her beau out to the cottage?" I said. "The weather's so beautiful. Maybe they've got nowhere to get away to for the weekend."

"You're right," Karel said. "Besides, everyone at the office is always saying how standoffish I am."

So the next day Karel went in and invited Jana and her beau out to our cottage on Sunday. Jana got all excited, said they'd be coming by motorcycle, and asked, By the way, how did they get to our place anyway?

"Oh, it's easy," Karel said. He took a sheet of paper with official letterhead and drew her out a map. "Now look, you go straight down Benešovská till you see this sign here for Ještěnice. Branch off to the left there, go straight down the local road, then over the bridge, and a little ways after that, on the right, you'll see two big buildings, right here. Past them's an intersection, take a left, and about two kilometers down the road, branch off again, this time to the right, then go down that, through the woods, like this, and after the woods you'll come to a village. On the left is a grocery store. Go around that, then the road curves back again toward the river. After that just keep going straight till you see the cottages. Here, I'll mark it for you: one, two, three. And that last one, the one that isn't finished yet, is ours. You'll be able to tell, since I'll be out there, covered in dust, laying down the concrete for the sidewalk. So try not to step in it, if you don't mind."

"Okay, thanks," Jana said. "My boyfriend's going to love it. We'll bring a bottle of something."

But they didn't bring anything. On Friday Jana didn't show up for work and Karel got word that she and her beau had been picked up by the police. It was a lousy weekend. We never did make it out to the cottage, and the sidewalk still wasn't done, since they came for Karel first thing Monday morning. They took him away and combed the whole place, turned the flat upside down, why and what for they didn't say.

Ten days later, a Wednesday, I got fired from the publishing house. I went home and sat in a daze, until somebody rang the bell and I opened the door to two dapperly dressed men with kissers like carved wood. They just flashed their IDs and said to come with them. I was about to ask for how long, but then thought better of it and instead said I had to go grab my handbag. One of the spooks slipped in behind me and kept an eye on my fingers as I dropped my wallet into my handbag along with my keys and a comb. A sudden chill came over me, so I went to the dresser for my wool vest, feeling his eyes on me at every step. He didn't stop gaping at me as I took the sweater from the drawer. I had half a mind to tell him I needed to go to the bathroom, but then realized he would probably just follow me right in.

As they escorted me down the stairs, one in front, one behind, it reminded me of the fairy tale: "Mist ahead and to the rear, let no one see, that I may hear." And wouldn't you know it, we had to run into Mrs. Bendová, coming home from doing the shopping. She put her bags down and stared so hard that I was surprised those owly eyes of hers didn't fall right out of her head. Just my luck. Five minutes later the whole building probably had me put away for ten years, assuming they hadn't just sent me straight to the gallows.

The dapper dans stuffed me into the back of a car waiting out front, one on my right, one on my left, and we sped off to Bartolomějská Street, headquarters of State Security. We got out of the car, one of them produced a key, unlocked a metal door on the side of the building, and shoved me inside. They followed me in and locked the door behind them. Then down a corridor to another door. Lock open, lock shut. Another corridor. Another door. Another lock. Mist ahead and to the rear. Five times in a row. I resigned myself to the thought that I would never see the light of day again as long as I lived.

When we came to the last door, they just knocked, pushed me inside, and disappeared. I found myself in an office that seemed about the size of my hand, along

with three men: one sitting at a typewriter, the second
at a small round table, and the third standing in the
corner by the door. Three pairs of eyes stuck to my
face like frog's feet. For a long time nothing happened.
Then the one at the table nodded to me to sit down
in the empty chair in the middle of the room. Then
nothing again. Precisely one second before I opened
my mouth and started to scream because I couldn't
breathe and it felt like the walls were collapsing in on
me and the room was moving like an elevator, the man
sitting across from me finally spoke. The typist tapped
at the keys. The man standing by the door staring
stood and stared.

"Do you know Antonín Fišer?"

Jesus, how long had those spooks practiced to be
able to make that stony face? I paid close attention
to these things. Even the blankest face betrayed some
emotion when it spoke. A normal human being just
can't talk without moving his face. Except for come-
dians in silent films, who make people laugh out loud,
and security police, who give people the creeps. What
did they look like at night when they got off their
shift, I wondered. You couldn't just casually stroll into
your neighborhood dive with a mask like that on and
say, "Waiter, please, a glass of red." My guess was they
stashed their faces in their lockers before they went

home from work, along with their service pistol, coffee mug, and bar of soap.

"Antonín Fišer?" I racked my brains. "I went to school with a Tonda Fišer. Dark-haired, stocky kid. Good soccer player. He died six years ago in a motor-cycle accident."

The typewriter rattled away.

"No, not him."

I thought so hard my head felt like it was going to burst, but nobody else came to mind. "If you could at least tell me when and where I'm supposed to know him from. I've met so many Fišers, I'm having a hard time remembering."

"You have a cottage near the Sázava river."

"We do. But there are no Fišers there. On our right we've got the Růžičkas and the Lukešes, on our left the Nejedlýs . . ."

"Antonín Fišer doesn't own a cottage. Did anyone ever come out to visit you?"

"Hardly ever. The cottage isn't finished, we just started on it in the spring. The only people we've invited have been the Čeněks and the Zemans, once, to help us out with the roof, and since then . . . just my husband's secretary, Jana Hronková—she was sup-posed to come, with her boyfriend. I never met him, though. I don't even know his name."

The man who'd been holding up the doorframe suddenly turned and walked out of the room. I assumed he was there to evaluate the officer leading the interrogation. He must have received at least a satisfactory, I guessed, considering he hit a bull's eye on the fourth question he asked.

I was stuck there in that hole for almost three hours. Finally the typist got up and left. When he came back he handed me four single-spaced sheets of paper to sign. I pretended to read them, but what with my head pounding and the letters swimming before my eyes, the truth was I had no idea what they said. At that point I would've gulped down a cup of hemlock if they'd given me one. And gladly. My God, if I was that beat after three hours of basically courteous questioning, I couldn't even imagine what Karel must have gone through!

They made sure to remind me that by signing I agreed not to mention our little conversation to anyone, and then it was back to the corridors with the doors and the locks. Only this time, when the last door slammed shut behind me, I was standing outside. It was still light out, and people were walking down the street, talking and laughing.

It took me two days to sort it all out in my head. That beau of Jana's really had been from out of town— West Germany, in fact. And when they collared him, he had Karel's map in his possession, showing how to get to our cottage. Those two big buildings Karel had so carefully diagrammed on the right-hand side after the bridge, before the turn to the left, well, it turned out they were military warehouses, or depots, or whatever you call them. Karel and I had driven by them almost every Saturday and it never even occurred to us—though it could have, since there was an army training ground in the woods that Karel had been so careful to include on the map, and who knew what else besides.

So that little map that Karel made for a Sunday afternoon visit turned him into a spy and me into an usher at the Horizon.

2

AT TEN THIRTY every night there was a sudden rise in decibels on the streets of Prague. People poured out of the cinemas talking up a storm to make up for their two hours spent in silence. Usually it had nothing to do with the film. Every now and then some fat lady with a perm would turn to her overweight balding husband and say: "Cripes, haven't we had enough of those war films already? Don't ever drag me to one of those things again," or, "Directors today are all over the place. They don't have the faintest idea," but most of the time they acted like people standing in line for customs after a trip out of the country: doing their best to talk about anything except what they had in their suitcase. Maybe tomorrow one of them would turn to their lover or spouse and say: "That was pretty good, right? How he set up that transmitter, right?" Or: "D'ja ever notice the legs on Bardot? Those are some fine-looking limbs, don't you think?" But for now they were just focused on not getting bruised during the steep descent back into reality.

The first usher to leave for home was Mrs. Kouřimská. As soon as the last ticketholder was out the door, she threw off her work smock, grabbed her handbag and dashed up the stairs, without so much as a glance in the mirror. Božena Šulcová, the salesgirl at the snack bar upstairs, was wiping down the counter with a damp cloth when Mrs. Kouřimská rapped on the glass with her ring. Looking up, the salesgirl saw her and came out from behind the counter, wobbling over to the door on aching legs.

"I'm sorry, Božena," Mrs. Kouřimská said, "but I don't suppose you have any leftovers? I'm afraid I haven't got even a slice of bread at home."

"Why, just look at you, Mrs. Kouřimská. You're thin as tissue paper, I can practically see right through you. You wait right there an' I'll wrap you up somethin'. Sorry no sweet rolls left, just some bread an', here we go, two frankfurters an' a slice of meatloaf. An' hold on, a little potato salad, toss that in a paper cup. That way you'll still have a bite for a snack tomorrow too. There, gimme five crowns for the whole shebang. It's all just scraps anyway."

Mrs. Kouřimská deposited the packages in her handbag and made her way out to the street. The sidewalks were as crowded as in the daytime. No one felt like going home in weather as nice as this. She didn't look around, but not much escaped Mrs. Kouřimská's notice. On a corner by the river, where the night air shimmered with the smell of the Vltava, a sharply angled silver head glittered beneath a streetlamp. The man stood on the curb, looking past her into the street at her back. She slowed her step and watched as the expression on his sun-browned face suddenly changed. Marie came running past and linked arms with the man. She twittered a few words, the silver-haired man laughed, and the two of them turned to walk down the stairs to the quayside. Reflected on the wall above their heads, as they sank lower and lower, a crooked-lettered inscription read: HE WHO DOESN'T LOVE HIS NEIGHBOR DESERVES AN ASS-KICKING.

Mrs. Kouřimská crossed the street to the bridge and quickened her stride. She came to a stop in a narrow lane, at an ancient building with a peeling façade. She climbed to the top floor, opened the door, switched on the lights, and set her bag down in a wardrobe in the entryway. She stepped into a six-cornered room with a dormer window affording a view of the city lights glimmering like the surface of the sea.

Mrs. Kouřimská opened a baroque chest, reached inside, turned a knob, and the sound of violins came soaring out like a phoenix. Circling her head as she entered the bathroom, with its cast-iron tub on lion's claws, the bird accompanied her as she reemerged, hair brushed and flowing down the back of a pink kimono embroidered with silver thread. She walked through the entryway into the kitchen. Opened the fridge and took a painted porcelain plate down from the shelf. Arranged a slice of truffle pâté, a dollop of crabmeat salad, and a hunk of French cheese on it. Stacked a few pieces of bread in a silver basket and removed a bottle of wine from the fridge. Sniffed the cork and poured some into a heavy baroque goblet. Spread a pink lace napkin on a tray with silver cutlery and carried it over to a small table beneath a lamp. Sat down in a pink brocade armchair that offered her a view of herself in a Venetian mirror adorned with glass flowers hanging on the opposite wall. Reached for the goblet, then suddenly stopped and got up. Went to the entryway and pulled the sacks of food that Božena had packed for her out of her handbag. Went back to the kitchen and threw them in the wastebasket. Finally, she settled back into the armchair, smiling at her reflection as she raised the goblet of wine. The windup clock on the console next to the window ticked away the minutes, the voice of the violins bubbling through the room. Mrs. Kouřimská laid her head against the chair's backrest and shut her eyes. The clock's little hand, wound round with metal decorated to look like lace, touched the Roman numeral one. The knocker on the front door clinked three times. Mrs. Kouřimská opened her eyes, smiled at the mirror again, inserted her toes into her silver slippers, and went to open the door.

3

"HOW MANY TIMES'VE I thought," Marie said, stretching. She clasped her hands behind her head and shut her eyes. "How many times've I thought, It isn't right, the two of us hookin' up like this. What with the circumstances and all . . . Poor Žofie's never gonna be the same again . . . She's like a body without a soul. And here I am with you . . . It just seems so wrong sometimes."

"Ah, c'mon. Grow up! What about all those people that got together during the war?"

"I know. It's just I'm so emotional . . . You know you shouldn't smoke so much, Václav . . . But isn't life just one big booby trap? You can't escape your destiny, even if—"

"Nah, I don't think so. Everyone decides his own—"

"Oh, gimme a break. What did Žofie decide? That two years after her wedding her husband would fall off the scaffolding and bust his neck? That some twisted madman would come along and murder her only child? Didn't you ever notice how some people got all the luck and the rest of 'em can't even catch a break if it falls right in their laps? How one day everything's comin' up roses and the next day it's bad news from the minute you get outta bed?"

"It's just coincidence."

"Coincidence, right. I remember back in school there was this girl, Alena Formánková. She'd only bone up on one page out of the whole book when we had a quiz, but you could bet money that was the one she'd get asked about. One time she just skipped the whole thing, didn't learn a word, and guess what? On her way to school the teacher sprained her ankle and had to go to the doctor's, so the test got canceled. Then my best friend, she had rotten luck from the day she was born. Her mother came from some backwater out in eastern Slovakia and loved romance novels, so she named her daughter Lionella. With a name like that, your life's bound to go off track. She was a great girl: nice-lookin', polite, always with her nose in the books, really knew her stuff. But she'd always get asked the one thing that slipped her mind, or came from some page her book was missing. Used to puke all over the bathroom, she got so nervous before every test. Now Alena's got a hunk of a husband, two perfect kids, and she's swimmin' in dough. Meanwhile Lionella's a teacher, lives with that wacky mother of hers, and I bet you she's still a virgin."

The man with the silver crew cut raised himself up on his elbow and with the other arm turned Marie to him. He glared at her so hard she flinched.

"Now you listen to me for a change," he said. "I'll tell you how it works. And no interrupting, got it?"

Marie nodded. He stretched out on his back again and stared up at the ceiling like the story of his life was being projected onto it.

"There were four of us kids at home and Pop was a baker. His whole life he looked forward to retiring and bein' able to sleep in like normal people do. Went to bed every day at five in the afternoon and got up at one-thirty in the middle of the night. But it wasn't enough to keep us fed, so my mom did people's laundry. We had a ramshackle cottage, down by the river in Bráník, where my mom scrubbed clothes on a washboard and bleached 'em out on the lawn. I was the oldest boy, so I helped her make deliveries. We'd pile the laundry in wicker baskets, load 'em onto the hay wagon and off we'd go. Uphill, I pushed. Downhill, I was the brakes. When we came to a customer's house, I'd grab one of the handles, my mom'd grab the other one and we'd lug the basket up the stairs. The lady of the house, or usually the maid, would take the clean laundry outta the basket, load the dirty in, and we'd lug it back down to our wagon. Then afterwards we'd hurry straight home, since one time we got jumped by some punk who took all our dough.

"Sometimes the ladies would slip me a piece of chocolate, which I'd just take and throw straight in the gutter, and their fancy-pants little boys would all come out and gawk at me like I was some circus monkey.

"But the worst part was my mom didn't even notice. She was just proud of how beautiful and white the laundry was and how satisfied all her customers were. But I made up my mind, back then, that someday I'd show 'em all."

The man propped himself up on his elbow again and turned to Marie.

"And look at me now," he said, almost menacingly. "Now I'm a somebody. Destiny's got nothin' to do with it. I made it happen. Work like a horse, follow orders . . ."

". . . serve the people." Marie couldn't resist.

"Damn right I do. You serve the people right, they stay in line and don't go gettin' ants in their pants . . ." The man paused a moment, seeming confused, then let out a hearty laugh. "Guess what happened the other day?" he said, then went ahead without waiting for an answer. "I ran into one of those highfalutin brats—if he lives to be a hundred, he'll always be a brat to me—anyway, he was one of the ones my mom used to do laundry for, and guess what he does now? Bustin' his hump in a bakery! Same one my dad worked at! Guy's got a PhD, I don't know what in. You should've seen the look on his face when I told him how far I'd come."

The man laughed again.

"It just takes a strong will. You gotta go for the goal and not muck around . . . Course," he added, "for a broad a lot depends on her looks. Good-lookin' broad's got everyone eatin' out of her hand."

"You're wrong about that," said Marie. "A pretty gal, I mean really pretty, doesn't have it easy. Other gals treat her mean 'cause they envy her looks, and guys treat her like a slut, since they're too jackassed to realize that just 'cause a gal's good-lookin' doesn't mean she wants to make it with them. So they get all jealous and make her life a livin' hell. Besides, looks don't mean a damn thing if you got rotten luck.

Take Helena, from work. Tall redhead? Don't try to tell me you never noticed or I'll smack you one in the jaw. Pretty as a picture, and educated too. And what's she got to show for it? Measles and smallpox. Hubby's in jail . . ."

"What for?" the man asked, reaching for another cigarette.

"What do I know? Some political thing. She never talks about it. It's even worse than bein' widowed or divorced. People steer clear of her, she's got no one to talk to . . ."

"How do you know? She might."

Marie snuggled up to him, wrapping one arm around his neck and pressing her lips to his muscular if overly hairy chest. Then she stretched out on her back again and said:

"Believe me, I know. You can't keep a secret at the Horizon. Anyway, if she did find somebody new, everyone'd badmouth her for runnin' around on her man in the clink. Meanwhile if the shoe was on the other foot and she was the one locked up, her husband would find another gal in a week and people'd say, 'What do you want, you can't expect him to be alone all that time.' Nobody expects a man to sacrifice. Pretty lousy deal, if you ask me."

"Well, woman is born to suffer, they say."

"Thanks a lot, you bastard. You should be ashamed of yourself. You don't even take me seriously."

"Don't I? You'd be surprised. I take you deadly seriously. I take everything seriously. It's an occupational hazard," the man said, stubbing out his cigarette on the glass top of the night table next to the overflowing ashtray.

"I'm not surprised your job makes you sick," said Marie. "But you can let down your guard with me, right? Now be a nice boy and tell me all about your day. How was it?"

Marie nestled her head against his shoulder and closed her eyes.

"Oh, you know," the man said in a sleepy voice. "Place is like a sinkin' ship. Nobody knows which hole to plug first. Today, for instance, we had a problem, real tough nut. But I cracked that thing wide open! Get this . . ."

Half an hour later he said: "I could use another drink. I'm thirstier than a fish outta water. Then I better skedaddle. Look what time it is."

Marie hopped out of bed and threw on a robe with a pattern of wildly colored flowers. By the time she came back with a bottle and a glass on a tray, Captain Nedoma was almost dressed.

"Good thing we're both such night owls and we

can sleep in in the morning," Marie said with a yawn. "What do you tell your wife when you come rollin' in late like this?"

"Nothing. What would I say? Workin' on a big case, that's about it. She knows I can't tell her the details."

"That's good. Whatever works. She never did understand you, anyway. Fella like you needs some sympathy, right? Meet me again tomorrow?"

"If you want."

"You dog. All right then. Tomorrow after the show, like always."

4

I HAD SUNDAYS off once a month, but instead of looking forward to them, they just filled me with dread. In the morning I would sleep in as late as I could, then clean my studio, even if there wasn't a speck of dust, wash my blouses and underwear, and then—what? If it was raining it was easy. "To hell with this life!" I'd say to myself. "On Sunday of all days it has to pour. Can't go out in weather like this." And take a book and snuggle up on the couch. The past few months I'd been reading so much that all those fictional lives on the page had begun to seem more real than my own. Sometimes I felt like there were too many books in the world, and that reading was a dangerous thing for someone like me. It gave you something beyond your own sad, lonely life, and though it acted as a protective shield, it could also be used as a wall or screen, a thing to hide behind. You could sit at home alone by the stove experiencing all these sensational things: loving, fearing, fighting, even dying, all in the space of one afternoon and three cups of coffee. Slowly you forgot that the story came from somebody's head, and you began to expect the same pattern and rules in real life as in books. You deluded yourself into thinking that after every exposition came a climax and a resolution, every episode fit into the overall arc of the narrative, and nothing happened without a purpose, since of course the story had to unfold smoothly and make some kind of sense. It was a dangerous drug. You began to see nothing but ambiguous symbols wherever you looked, interpreting everything from the perspective of some higher plan, forgetting that if there actually was any order in the world, it was created by an intelligence too sophisticated for human beings to comprehend. If we want to get by in life, we need to just concentrate on keeping our heads above water and stop wondering why things happen all the time. *Maybe God really is the Great Surveyor, who drew up the plans and built this maze we scuttle around in clueless as mice, running up against His laws at every turn. Of course none of us stand a chance of figuring out which path leads where. The only way to run in the right direction is by accident.*

So on Sundays when it rained cats and dogs, I'd sit happily at home, devouring the books I brought home from the library, snorting them up like cocaine. But the weather this Sunday was gorgeous, and if I didn't get out at least for a while my head would start to pound, and by nighttime I'd feel wrung out as a dishrag. *All right, I'll go for a walk. You never know, something nice might happen to me. They should ban Sundays for lonely people.*

It was crowded down by the river, mostly couples, some with children. *If they let Karel out in six years, best-case scenario, I'll be thirty. Is that too late for a baby? Supposedly you should have your first kid by thirty, tops.*

Old ladies, dressed in their Sunday best, white hair tinted blue, pattered into the Mánes café for their weekly coffee and cake.

Everyone's afraid of old age, I thought, *and meanwhile those old grannies are happier than any of us. They've done their time. Nobody expects anything of them anymore. At last they can stop spending their lives chasing after happiness. Or at any rate stop looking for it in places that are out of reach and hard to pin down, and instead find it in things they can find and enjoy every day—a good meal, a sit in the sun, an absence of suffering.*

Now that half the afternoon was shot, what was I going to do with myself? I could call Růžena, but of course she liked to spend Sundays alone with her husband. Pity my life wasn't a book. In a classic Russian novel I would reside in a village with my rich relatives, and on a day like today I'd be out on the veranda, shooing away the wasps while I stirred a kettle of preserves. Or maybe I'd have a cozy little room on the waterfront and sit writing notes to deranged yet compassionate gentlemen, who would come rushing straight to see me, but one way or another they'd be foiled every time, so no matter how much haste they made they would never arrive. A French author, on the other hand, would most likely install me in some Left Bank dive, where I would proceed to engage in casual conversation with a fascinatingly neurotic married man, followed by a trip to the south—ravishing yet fraught with intimations of a creeping alienation. And, finally, as a young Manhattanite I would climb into a cab and be off to a cocktail party, drink myself silly and wake up the next day in a strange flat with one man shaving, another man playing guitar, and everyone talking the way nobody ever does in real life, every sentence a laugh riot, or worse. Whatever kind of book it was, *something* would have happened.

If only at least I would run into someone. One of

the girls from school, say. Even if it was the stupidest bimbo in the whole class. Even Magda Krupičková. I bet she'd stop and talk to me. Lord, was I that bad off that I'd even talk to her?

Dammit, my feet hurt. I should've stayed at home. What was I looking for out on the street? What did I expect to find? What good could come of it? I just needed to come to terms, once and for all, with the fact that this was my life and it wasn't going to change. This was what it was going to be like, year in, year out, and if I couldn't learn to cope on my own, I was going to go out of my mind. Karel would come home to a nutcase.

What was I going to do now, though? Let's try and be systematic, I thought. Things I could do: 1) Go see a play. Sure, assuming I had the dough and assuming there were any tickets left. 2) Call some friends. Right. They'd say, "Helena, how are you? We have to get together sometime. I'll give you a ring next week." 3) Go out for dinner. Sounded all right, except for the fact that eating dinner alone in some dive would be even worse than eating alone at home. 4) See an art show, only now it was too late, and besides, my feet hurt too much. Dammit, I should've thought of that sooner. I could've gone to see those Navrátil paintings up at the Castle. At least I had my schedule figured out for next week. Or 5) Just go home and read. Kick off my shoes, get undressed, take a bath, and climb into bed with a book.

It wasn't so bad being alone, actually. How many smart people had fled into the wilderness or locked themselves up in a tower, just to get away from people? So what? Everyone treats each other so badly, and besides, what was there really to say? At least when you were alone you could think. You didn't have to make small talk or worry about anyone stabbing you in the back. It was great being alone. Nobody bugged me and I could do whatever I wanted. In fact it was so great I had to stop thinking about it or I was going to break down in tears right there on the street.

Next chance I got, I was going to have to ask a psychologist why it felt so important to talk to people. Why was it that sometimes even the best book couldn't take the place of a human voice? Why did I feel like the day wouldn't be such a waste if I were to bump into someone right now and exchange a few pointless words?

Some families with children stood on Jirásek Bridge. The children were tossing crumbs of bread to the gulls, who performed feats of acrobatics to show their gratitude. "Daddy," one of the little boys asked, "don't those gulls look like great big butterflies?"

Maybe it didn't matter so much what people said to each other. The reason we talk isn't to share nuggets of wisdom, but to pause a moment in our flight through life, to make a connection, reassure ourselves we've got something in common—a human word, a human voice. Also, when you talk to another person, you think differently than when you talk to yourself. Maybe words, any at all, directed to someone else, are an act of love in a way. When I talk to you, I enter your life and you enter mine. We share our worlds with each other. It isn't just that we need a living screen to project ourselves on. The truth is we all have things inside us that aren't real till we share them with somebody else. It wouldn't be hard for me to believe that a lonely woman sleeps with a man less for sex than to have him talk to her. And that whatever he tells her means a lot more and sticks in her memory longer than the night the two of them spend in bed.

I couldn't betray Karel by leaving him. Even if I couldn't help him, the least I could do was wait. Faithfully and stupidly. I knew how much he needed me to be here when he returned, and to be the same woman I was when he left. But could I? Was that even possible? Can a woman preserve herself like fruit? What if everything he loved most about me withered up and died? Usually when people thought about the future, what they feared was physical aging. That wasn't what I was afraid of. A woman at thirty is still good-looking. Inside, on the other hand, she can change enormously, to the point of no return. And what about Karel, how would he change? *Dear God,* I prayed, *please bring him back as soon as you can!* If only there was something I could do—anything at all.

Well, hurray, home at last. I was whipped.

I entered the building and pressed the button on the wall to call the elevator. As it arrived and the door slid open, somebody else walked in the entrance. I stepped into the car, rested a finger on the button marked 5, and called back over my shoulder:

"Are you coming up?"

"Gladly, with your permission!" a man's voice replied.

I turned to look.

The man stood in the doorway, illuminated from behind. The only thing I could make out was the smile on his face. "I've been following you all afternoon," he said.

He took a few steps forward and put his hand in the elevator door to keep it from closing.

"And why might that be?"

"That isn't hard to guess. The bigger mystery is how come a girl like you is walking the streets all alone on a Sunday afternoon. If you don't mind, I'd like to invite you to dinner. And maybe you could tell me a little about yourself."

"I'd appreciate it if you went away. And let go of the door. I'm sorry you wasted your afternoon."

The man turned serious. "Please, hear me out. I realize this isn't the proper way to introduce myself and I don't mean to offend you. But this is ridiculous. If you take that elevator right now, I'll probably never see you again. And that would be a shame. Two lonely people like us, we might get along really well."

"Actually, you're mistaken. I'm a married woman."

"Happily?"

"Very much so."

"I'm sorry, but I don't believe you. A happily married woman doesn't spend her Sunday afternoon walking the streets till she drops. People who've got somebody waiting at home for them don't do that. Look, I'm no bum. I'm a decent man. My name is Šípek. Jaromír Šípek. I'm a zoologist. I can tell you all kinds of amazing stories about monkeys and elephants. You like animals? Would you like to go to the zoo next Sunday? How about dinner?"

"I adore animals. But I'm busy next Sunday and I'll

be having dinner at home. Now, since you're a decent man, please let go of the door. I'm tired. Good-bye."

The door closed. I pressed the button and the elevator started up.

5

"ALL RIGHT, SHOOT. What's the story? What's the news?" The man, sprawled comfortably in an armchair, lifted his glass of beer.

"Nothing. Not a thing. Doesn't mix with anyone. Nobody calls her. Doesn't say a word unless she has to. Hard to believe."

"You can say that again. Piece of skirt like that, she must have guys crawlin' all over her. We need to know *everything*. I hope I make myself clear."

"She doesn't mix with anyone at the cinema. I haven't taken my eyes off her."

"It just doesn't add up. There's something missing.

We've just got to stay on top of it, take the bull by the horns. With the right strategy, we'll get results. That's my experience."

"Well, you can't blame me. I'm doing my job."

"I know you're trying. But you need the right approach. If the work isn't based on the right approach—look, just the fact that she keeps her distance from everyone is suspicious. Fišer sang like a bird. The messages go through the cinema. He was supposed to pick 'em up there on Monday after we collared him. But he claims not to know who from or how, and I almost believe him. It's standard practice in this line of work. No one knows more than they have to."

"Well, one thing for sure is, a cinema's the ideal spot. With a couple hundred people around, who can keep track of them all at once?"

"True, only this time we got lucky and also bagged Karel Novák. Talk about a hardhead. We can't get a thing out of him. Not for lack of tryin', mind you. Couple years ago, we'd have squeezed it out of him easy. We have our ways. Scientifically tested and proven. Not anymore, though. Goddam job. How're we supposed to get results with our hands tied behind our backs? Fišer had Novák's map on him and I don't believe in coincidence. Novák's wife had to be in on it too, it's only logical, and sooner or later she's going to lead us to someone."

"Well, that was a smooth move getting her in the Horizon. She pounced on it like a wildcat. Sure, it looks suspicious, but it might not mean anything. When a gal's man is in the clink, she's happy to take the first job that comes along. But any way you slice it, I've got nothing to report."

"Well, see to it that you do. And pronto. Remember, sweetie, you've got a lot to lose. I've been satisfied in the past, but things're dragging a bit this time. And when I say you've got a lot to lose, I don't mean just this flat."

"This is a special case. I can't figure that Helena out. But this much I know: Nobody's contacted her on the job. And the moment she steps out the door, it's not my business anymore. The cinema's my turf."

"That kid's murder fouled everything up. As soon as the public gets wind of these things, and especially the police, the plants run for cover—it blows the whole thing. But I still think the Horizon was too sweet a setup for them to kiss it good-bye. Maybe we just need to give it some time. Hey, don't suppose you got another beer in there?"

"You bet. Comin' right up."

The man drank thirstily, then pushed his glass aside. Instinctively he lowered his voice.

"I've got a plan to make some headway on this thing. Nothing fancy, easy to carry out, but it'll take some organizing." As he spoke, he rapped the tabletop with an angular index finger. "We can nail this thing if I get it right, but it's going to take some work. Give me a week, maybe ten days. If you haven't dug up anything new by then, we'll give it a go. I'll stop by again next week. There's no such thing as an innocent person. Get that through your head. You can't see it till you look. But as soon as you do, everything about 'em, everything they do, is suspicious. That's the way to look at it."

"You bet. You can count on me. I'll take care of it. That's what I'm here for."

"That's all I ask." The man drew a long yellow envelope from his breast pocket and laid it on the table next to the empty half-liter glass. "This isn't a Christmas present, got it? We expect results. You've got a lot to lose," he repeated.

He stood up, looked around the room, and walked out the door without a good-bye.

The woman, still seated, shut her eyes. After a while, she stood up, took the envelope from the table and tucked it, still unopened, under a pile of paper napkins in the drawer.

6

⁓

". . . O H S U R E , I understand, no need to explain,
I know how much work you have . . . Don't worry
about it . . . Right, I'll call again when I get a chance . . .
Bye now."

I hung up the phone and went back to my table.

That was the third time now Růžena had said she
didn't have time. And she hadn't called in at least a
month. If not longer.

"You all right?" the waitress asked airily.

"Yes, just feeling hot. Could you bring me a glass of
seltzer please? And another cup of coffee."

"You know you really shouldn't smoke. By the third month it'll pass. When I was—"

"Oh, it's nothing. I'm just a little dizzy. Could you bring me that seltzer please?"

"Fine. Young people today. You won't take a word of advice."

I should be ashamed of myself. Jesus, what was the matter with me? So Růžena had dumped me. So what? I had to give her credit for not doing it sooner. What would we have done if we'd gotten together, anyway? I wasn't exactly a barrel of laughs, not to mention I was broke. I felt like the fifth wheel wherever I went. It couldn't have been too nice having a walking disaster like me around when your life was going the way you wanted. I also kept forgetting I was dangerous to be seen with. Růžena's husband couldn't have been too thrilled about our friendship. He was trying to build a career. What if people found out, which they certainly would, who his wife was palling around with? God knows how long he'd been telling her to ditch me already. That must have been it. He put the knife to her throat and she gave in. What woman is going to break up her marriage over a friend?

And why should she? If I could get by without Karel, I could do without Růžena too. Of course, then I really didn't have anyone left to talk to. The two of us had been friends for as long as I could remember. Heck, we went to high school together. Skating on the patch of ice out in back of school, then at the rink on Štvanice Island. School dances. Couples trips on weekends, hiking in the mountains . . . those beautiful nights stirring the goulash over the fire while the boys set up the tents. Nothing left to do now but cry my eyes out. Mrs. Comrade Marek Štancl was no longer a part of my life. Maybe she'd cave in and get back in touch. No. There was no use kidding myself. Unless I wanted to ruin my nights waiting at home for the phone to ring. Only time it ever rang anymore was by mistake. Might as well have the thing disconnected. What was the point of a phone that didn't ring? A friend who never had time? A life where nothing ever happened?

What a silly goose I am. Here my husband is in jail and I'm carrying on over a friend. Over the fact that I'm now completely, utterly alone.

Being alone wasn't that bad, though. It was just a matter of habit. There were all kinds of things I could do. I could go wherever I wanted. Cafés, art galleries, concerts. Not like the Jews during the war. They weren't allowed to go anywhere. Now *that* was being alone. I could stroll around the city, or go out of town for the weekend. See the horse races in Chuchle. Take a steamboat down the Vltava . . .

Dammit, I didn't do anything wrong, and if people avoided me that was their loss—and *voilà*, right back where I started. The bottom line was I could stand anything, as long as I knew I was innocent. But did it actually matter? If they executed an innocent man, was he any less dead for it? Was dying any easier for him than for the man who could say, "I may've gone wrong, but I own up to what I did. I deserve my punishment"? Wasn't it better to pay a price, however outrageous, for a reason than to suffer for no reason at all?

Enough. When thoughts like that started to come over me, it was time to pull up anchor before I drowned in the sea of my own stupidity. I would walk to work and try to think about something truly important, like how to cut the fabric for that indigo-print skirt so I'd still have enough left over for pockets.

MATINEES TENDED TO be half full at best. Most of the audience was school-age kids who weren't allowed to go to evening screenings or, on the other hand, old folks who didn't like to go out at night. Five minutes into the show, Helena ushered a limping elderly lady to the twelfth row, tucked her flashlight back in her pocket, and exited to the lobby. For the next two hours she was more or less free. She decided to head to the office to write up a report for the manager. As she passed the concession stand, she heard another late-comer walking down the stairs. Mechanically she spun around, strode back to the theater entrance, and held out her hand for the ticket. The man reached gingerly into his upper jacket pocket, lifted out a crumpled bou-quet of violets, and laid them in Helena's outstretched palm. She looked up at him in surprise, then immedi-ately frowned.

"Mr. Šípek, what on earth do you think you're doing?"

"You mean, why would I come to see such a corny film? I swear, I wouldn't dream of it. I came to see you."

"How did you know I worked here?"

"I'll tell you if you promise not to be mad. Will you be mad?"

Helena shook her head.

"Well, the truth is, I did a little investigating à la Sherlock Holmes. Your neighbor was overjoyed that your cousin from Bechyně had come to visit, and directed me straight here. Of course now you're going to get angry and send me packing. This is the biggest risk I've ever taken in my life. Look, my knees are shaking. Would you mind if we sat down somewhere?"

Helena looked around uncertainly.

"Here, come into the smoking lounge, but just for a minute. We can't let my boss see us. She runs a tight ship."

They went into the corner of the smoking lounge, where they couldn't be seen from the hallway, and sat there in silence for several minutes. Finally, Helena said sternly:

"Look, Mr. Šípek, I think the best way to get rid of you is to level with you about my situation. Then you'll leave me alone and we'll both be better off for it. You see, I'm not your average case. Any law-abiding citizen who cares about his reputation wouldn't touch me with a ten-foot pole."

"Now wait a minute. First let me speak my piece. And for God's sake, don't get upset. You see, once I found out what your name was and where you worked, it wasn't hard to get the rest. I know about your husband. Not every detail, of course—just the overall situation. I have to admit, when I first saw you on Sunday, like any man I thought you were one fine girl and I'd be crazy if I didn't at least try to get to know you. I'm not going to lie about how shaken I was when I found out what had happened. It made me think about certain things—including myself—for the first time in my life."

He paused a moment.

"Look, plain and simple, I came to ask if you might need—well, a friend. A kindred spirit, nothing more. Really. Instead of wandering the streets we could take a trip on Sunday. I've got an old clunker, a real museum piece, but it still runs. Or we could go see a play. Whatever you want."

Helena turned the crumpled bouquet in her fingers.

"I promise to be on my best behavior. Just so you know I mean it, I won't come by again. I'll leave you my phone number, and you can call if you want to see me. Here's my number at home. I also have an office at the zoo— just a shack, really, that I share with one of my coworkers. At night we like to sit around and drink tea with rum—it's delicious. If you ever feel like dropping by, I can introduce you to the lion. Here's that number."

He rose from his seat and looked down at Helena's bowed head. Halfway to the door, he stopped and turned around: "One more thing. Don't think I'm trying to help you. I need you to help me. By coming by every once in a while to sit and have a chat."

Helena stared dully at the door as it swung on its hinges, trying to remember what she had been doing before he arrived. She stood up, walked into the office, and tucked the violets in with the bouquet of primroses poking out of the vase on the manager's desk.

"I found them. Somebody threw them out," she said as the manager looked up in bewilderment.

"Hey, Helena," Marie said as the two of them walked upstairs after the night's last screening. "Instead of heading straight home, what do you say we go grab a coffee over at Slavia?"

Helena was stunned. None of her coworkers had ever shown any interest in personal conversation with her. That made the second person today who was willing to waste their time on her. A downright mob compared to the usual.

She eyed Marie suspiciously, but then nodded. "All right. But not for too long. I'm pretty worn out."

As they stepped into the café, Marie headed straight for a small table for two, half-hidden behind a column. *She isn't exactly thrilled to be seen with me*, Helena sighed to herself.

As usual at that time of night, Slavia served as a quiet haven for refugees from empty homes. A few elderly men stared doggedly into their newspapers, as if by sheer force of will they could conjure up something worth reading, while three or four women sat scattered around the café, alone at their tables, desperately bored yet refusing to call it quits, write off another day, and return home to their private, unaccompanied solitude.

"Damn, it's really hoppin' tonight," said Marie. "Place is about as lively as an undertakers' convention. At least those girls over there look like they're havin' fun."

In the middle of the coffeehouse, seated around four tables pushed together, was a gathering of women who looked to be in their thirties, dolled up like fashion models in sparkling dresses, with accessories in matching colors. Any woman who couldn't make the grade had clearly stayed at home. Easily outshining them all, though, was a sunny blonde with dimpled cheeks and a plain black sweater with a seemingly bottomless neckline, expertly designed to display her dazzling cleavage. Hunched on the chair next to her, by contrast, was a bony brunette with a bad complexion and squinty eyes, dressed in a radiant bright-beige suit and a silk blouse, which she kept unbuttoning and buttoning to ensure the blazer's perfect cut was employed to maximum effect. The group of ladies chattered away excitedly, every now and then bursting into a fit of giggles.

"College reunion," Helena said. "Bragging about how far they've come in the past ten years."

"And showin' the world they're still as young and stupid as ever," sneered Marie.

A ginger-haired waitress shuffled unsteadily up to their table and thunked two cups of thick white porcelain down in front of them. Marie rescued two soggy lumps of sugar from the puddle of coffee in her saucer, dropped them in the cup, and stirred her spoon distractedly.

"So, Helena," she said, laying her spoon back on the marble tabletop. "I hope you don't think I'm tryin' to butt into your personal business."

She thought a moment, resettled herself in her chair, and started over.

"No, that's not it. What I mean is: I *am* tryin' to butt into your personal business, but I hope it won't upset you."

Helena stared back at her, but didn't reply.

"Now look," Marie went on. "One thing: Next time you wanna have a chat with someone in the smoking lounge, sit about two chairs farther down to the right. Otherwise, from the cloakroom we can hear every word. I donno if there's a hole in the partition or what, but seriously, it's like you're talkin' into a megaphone. So obviously we all went runnin' in today to hear lover boy there try to woo you. Ládinka practically started bawlin' she was so moved. I just thought you should know, so maybe next time you can watch out for it. So that's number one. Do you mind? If you do, just say so. Or can I go on?"

"Why, of course," Helena said with some hesitation. "I'm very grateful. It's kind of you to bring it to my attention."

"Well, we'll see if you're still grateful when you hear what I have to say next." Marie smiled and lit a cigarette. "You know, I've been watchin' you a long time, Helena, and sometimes it makes my head spin. You call that a life? You hardly talk to anyone. It's like you're a nun or something."

"Try to understand, Marie. What am I supposed to do? I have no way to help my husband . . ."

"Exactly. If you can't help him, why not at least help yourself? Look, Helena, don't think I don't get it. You're in a tough spot, so you made up your mind you gotta do everything perfect from now on. It's like a superstition: As long as I'm a good girl, everything'll turn out all right. I know what that's like."

Marie wrinkled her forehead and nodded knowingly.

"But you wanna be happy too, don't you? What's the point of life otherwise? Am I right?" Marie said, leaning across the table.

"Look, Marie," Helena said. "Until Karel comes home, the only thing that can make me happy is to renounce all happiness without regret. I've made my peace with that."

"All right," Marie said with a note of disgust. "You

wanna play the martyr, burning at the stake? That's a way to be happy too, I guess."

"Well, I'm far from being a martyr, I think."

"I sure hope so. But how can you actually tell what's the right thing to do? Who decides that? People who don't have a clue what you're goin' through? God in Heaven? Look, I'm not the most religious gal. The only time I normally set foot in church is when I'm up the creek, but basically I believe there has to be a God, since I can't do without Him, just like I can't do without food. But I don't really think He meant all those commandments literally. I mean, there's no way God could want me to honor the father that He gave me in all his grace and mercy. There must've been some misunderstanding. And there's lots of things like that. So do I think we can count on Him a hundred percent? No. We each gotta figure it out for ourselves, and of course we're gonna screw up all sorts of things along the way."

Marie crushed out her cigarette and poked the butt around in the ashtray a while. Then she rummaged through her bag, pulled out another one, lit it up, and frowned earnestly.

"You know," she said, "if you ask me, it's a mistake to try to be perfect. People are human and that's how they gotta live. Not like devils, but not like angels either. The only place an angel can make it's in Heaven."

"You're quite the philosopher," Helena said in amazement. "I never would've guessed . . ."

". . . that I could keep more than one thing in my head at a time? See, that's just it. Nobody can keep their mind on one thing. This life we got is complicated. The world's full of hate and dirty tricks, and tryin' to be some innocent saint isn't gonna save you. I know I'm just a simple working girl compared to you. I never went to college. But I bet I could teach you a thing or two about life."

Marie wearily propped her elbows on the table and sighed. "I know I don't know how to say things like I'd like to. But what I'm tryin' to get at is this: Those people that live like saints usually make their lives into hell. But the worst part is, they also screw it up for everyone else, since they're so saintly and innocent they don't know how to deal with the world. Sometimes I think if it wasn't for them it wouldn't be so easy for the actual bad guys. Are you listenin' to me, Helena? Do you understand? C'mon, say something!"

"I'm listening," said Helena. "And I think I understand. But it isn't so easy for me. I can't just change my skin like a reptile."

"Yeah, I know that. But open up your eyes a little. I'd hate to see you go off the deep end tryin' to do the right thing."

"The truth is, lately I've had the feeling . . ." Helena began, but she was interrupted by an outburst of laughter. The women at the reunion were cackling so loudly that the elderly man at the neighboring table lifted his head from his newspaper and peered at them admonishingly over his glasses. The pretty blonde, catching his look, gave a boisterous yelp and, without turning her head, elbowed her neighbor who was just lifting a full glass of Bikavér from the table. Traveling in a high arc, the red wine landed on the precious fabric of the woman's beige suit and bled into a stain shaped like a giant red octopus. The whole table froze as the blonde covered her gaping mouth with a tanned hand. The woman in the suit sat motionless, her hand suspended halfway between the table and her face. Then, slowly and deliberately, almost triumphantly, she tipped the glass upside down, emptying the rest of the wine onto her skirt. Then she turned her head, her icy gray eyes drilling into the blonde's face, set the glass on the table, stood up, lifted her handbag from the back of her chair, and strode stiffly toward the door.

"Did you see how worn-down her heels were?" Marie whispered to Helena. "I bet she forked out so much for that suit she didn't have any leftover for shoes. Who knows how long she scrimped and saved to be able to show that blonde bitch."

The waiter appeared at the women's table. He pulled his wallet from his pocket, shook it open, pressed the tip of his pencil to his notepad, and made a face so earnest his eyebrows blended into the shock of hair combed over his forehead. One by one the women opened their purses, paid, and rose from the table as quickly and quietly as possible. They filed out of the café like geese. None of them said a word. Life wasn't such a laugh anymore. In fact it wasn't even worth talking about.

"Some party," Marie said as the door closed behind them. "Camaraderie's a beautiful thing. Are you as worn-out as I am?" she said with a loud yawn. "I'm flat as a five-day-old beer. Tell me, though. Do you mind my preachin' to you like that? Still friends? Cross your heart?"

"Of course," said Helena. "I really appreciate your being so concerned about me."

"Guess it's time we got outta here," Marie said, looking languidly around the café.

The waiter was already on his way to their table. From up close, his face looked puffy and debauched, and his beautifully groomed quiff of hair was run through with gray.

7

SHORTLY AFTER NOON the doorbell rang. Marie removed the three curlers over her forehead, threw on her robe, and opened the door to a stout middle-aged woman in a gray dress suit.

"Hello, I'm Mrs. Nedomová," the woman said with a pleasant smile. Marie unwittingly backed away. The woman stepped in the door and walked through the entryway into the living room. She paused a moment to survey the scene, then made straight for Marie's prize armchair. She lifted a bra hanging off the arm by its strap, picked up a lone stocking from the floor, looked around the room

again, and laid them both on the couch. Then she settled into the armchair, opened her handbag, and took
out a pack of cigarettes.

"Please, Miss Vránová, won't you have a seat?"
the woman said, still with the same pleasant smile.
"Smoke?" She offered her cigarettes.

Marie slumped dully onto the couch.

"I've been planning to visit for quite some time, you
know. I wanted to ask how you're hitting it off with my
husband. You've been seeing each other a few months
now. Don't you think it's time you tied the knot?" Mrs.
Nedomová stood up and removed the ashtray full of
butts from the pile of junk on the night table. "He
really shouldn't smoke so much," she noted drily. She
rested the ashtray on the arm of the chair and sat back
down.

"You have to admit—it's hardly a life: meeting in
secret, an hour or two a day, when you could have your
own home, a family even, vacations—the whole kit
and caboodle. What do you say?"

Marie just sat silently.

"Now listen carefully, miss. I just popped out of the
office for a moment and can't stay long. So let's settle
this thing right now. I've come in all sincerity to offer
you my husband's hand. Look. I've been with him
nineteen years. He's gone through so many young

ladies in that time I'd need a card catalog to keep track
of them all. I was eighteen when I married Václav. I
knew as much about life as a horse knows about holy
water. Next thing I knew I had two little kids and
things weren't so simple anymore. Once or twice a
year I'd get up the courage to say maybe we should get
a divorce, but he would always act so surprised and
offended, and say how sorry he was, that I gave up.
He couldn't understand why I wasn't happy. After
all, he was a good looking guy, brought home the
bacon, was respected at work. When I mentioned
the young ladies, he was appalled that I'd be so petty
as to break up the family and take our kids' father
away over such a silly thing. He wouldn't hear of it.
And so on it went. He did what he wanted, I did
what he wanted, and our happiness was complete.
When he came home at the end of the day, all worn
out from one of his dates, I was right there waiting
for him, the whole flat spick-and-span, shirts washed
and ironed, socks darned, so he'd always look sweet as
a rose for the ladies."

She paused to shoot a questioning glance at Marie,
as if expecting her to acknowledge what a devoted wife
she had been. But Marie just sat there. Mrs. Nedomová
leaned in toward her and continued in a confidential
tone:

"There's nothing really manly about these Don Juan types at all, you know. They're just little boys who refuse to grow up. They want to romp around the sandbox, then go home to their mommy who adores and admires them, even if they're still peeing their pants at fifty. That's why so few of them are bachelors, even though it would seem to make sense from a logical point of view. But they can't bear the thought of living without their mommy, waiting for them with open arms even when they're drunk as a skunk. Young ladies come and young ladies go, but a mother's love is forever. Anyway, to cut to the chase, Miss Vránová, my daughters are growing up, so I think it's high time my little boy found himself a wife. You've been with him long enough to fill my shoes, so I can go into retirement and take care of myself for a change. I've got a good job, decent pay. I could even afford to chip in assuming you managed to swing it so that he married you and gave me a divorce on good terms. He wouldn't have to know a thing. He's a handsome man, high status—you could end up with worse. He is getting on in years. It's a tiring lifestyle, you know? But marriage is a serious matter, I realize, you need to think it through. Just think quick. This is a solid offer and if you don't make up your mind soon, I'll go look somewhere else. Here's the phone number to my office, so let me know. Good-bye for now. If we make a deal

soon, for your wedding I'll get you one of those rugs
from the hard currency stores."

She laid her calling card on the table, stood up,
scanned the room one more time, smiled sweetly again,
and walked out the door.

Marie just sat staring at the ground a while. Finally
she took a deep sigh, got up, and opened the wardrobe. First she dug out a hard cardboard box from the
bottommost shelf and a pair of slightly worn men's slippers. She took a checkered bathrobe and two yellowing
shirts from the hangers. She went to the bathroom and
brought out a small pile of toiletries, then took everything and packed it up in the box. She wrapped the
box in a piece of crumpled wrapping paper and tied it
with string. She carefully wrote the address out in big
block letters, put the box in a string bag, and laid it on
the table. She would stop off at the post office on her
way to work tomorrow.

Helena and Šípek exited through the zoo side gate.
The staff had already locked the main entrance, all
of the visitors were long gone, and the twilight rang
with the excited shrieks of animals being fed.

"You think they're sad?" Helena asked. "You think
they wish they were free?"

"Not most of them, I don't think. Experts agree that animals are almost like people when it comes to that. As long as they've got a nice place to live and something to keep them entertained, they can do without freedom. In a good zoo, where they're well-fed and have a chance to socialize, most animals are happier than they would be, as one scholar put it, in lonely and dangerous freedom."

They reached the parking lot, where a boxy Tatra, three or four years older than Helena, sat waiting. It had been ingeniously patched up, stitched together, and coated in a lacquer of the finest burgundy. Its owner had clearly expended a tremendous amount of love and care on it, over the course of many years. Šípek proudly opened the door and helped Helena climb inside. He settled in behind the wheel, seeming a little nervous, but the engine fired on the fourth turn of the key.

"There. Now let's go for dinner. I know a nice little pub by the river. The schnitzels there are so big they don't even fit on your plate. We can sit under a tree in the garden and have a beer. That's my idea of perfect bliss right now. But, say, I'm not tiring you out or boring you with all my talk, am I?"

"Me?" Helena laughed. "I can't remember the last time I had such a nice afternoon. I'd even given up on the idea that it was possible."

"Why wouldn't it be? It's possible every Sunday you have off. And other things are possible too. Next time I can borrow a boat from my friend and row you down to Bráník . . ."

"Oh no. Not a chance. You're too nice. I would just be taking advantage of you. But thank you so much for today. It's been lovely. You know, otherwise I would have just . . ."

"I know. It's been a lovely day."

There were only four tables in the garden at the riverside pub. At one of them sat an elderly couple, the man in a yellow open-necked shirt, a little pinched around the waist, the woman squeezed into a blue-and-white-striped cotton dress. Both of them had rosy cheeks, pale blue eyes like geese, and white hair. They sat silently over their half-liter mugs, radiating peace and contentment like heat from a stone. As Helena took the last bite of her enormous schnitzel and lifted her eyes from the plate, she saw the man put his hand on top of his wife's and stroke her wrinkled skin. Without even exchanging a glance the two of them smiled, as if at some long-ago memory.

I wonder if someday that will be me and Karel, Helena thought.

"It's so nice here, isn't it?" she said quickly, her voice slightly hoarse. "I just love summer nights. When I was little, we lived in an old block of flats with a balcony. A huge acacia tree grew out in front, and in summer sometimes I would sneak out to the balcony at night and sit huddled up in my nightgown. The acacia smelled gorgeous, and I would listen to the birds with their nest in there, cheeping away."

"Just wait till we get out on the water sometime. When it gets dark we can pull ashore and make a little fire. Evening on the river is truly a thing of beauty, you'll see. Everything will collapse someday. Buildings, bridges, machines—it can all disappear in seconds, but the elements—water, earth, air, fire—those are what will remain. Sitting by a campfire on the river, it's like rubbing up against eternity for a while."

The first gusts of cool wind off the river rustled the treetops. The bells in the church on the hilltop sounded quietly, as if they too were swaying in the breeze.

Helena bent her head over the red checkered tablecloth. "I'm sure it would be wonderful. But try to understand, I can't. Karel is my man, my one and only, I'm closer to him than anyone else in the world. And he's in such a jam. Every morning when I get out of bed and see my clean white sheets I feel like a traitor. When I sit down to a nice lunch, I wonder what gives me the right to live this way when Karel . . . At first I couldn't stop thinking about how to help him. Now I've made my peace with the fact there's nothing I can do. Except wait."

"Maybe the best way to help him is to live as normally as possible. I sometimes try to imagine how I would feel in Karel's place. What I would expect from my wife. And I know I wouldn't want her to worry herself to death before I got back."

"But you probably also wouldn't want her sitting around a campfire by the riverside with another man," Helena laughed.

"That's the question," Šípek said. "Most of all, I think I would want her to be well, for both our sakes. It goes without saying how much I would hope she waited for me and didn't find someone else in the meantime." He paused, looked into Helena's eyes, and gave a sad little grin. "But I wouldn't want her to forsake all pleasure. To make her life a prison sentence out of loyalty to me. It's just that—it's hard to say what a person would think in a situation he can't even imagine. And an even bigger question is whether what a person thinks or wants can be binding on anyone else. After all, whether we like it or not, we decide for ourselves. And we shouldn't do to ourselves what we would never dream of doing to somebody else."

"I'll think about it," Helena said. "Really."

It was just the two of them in the little garden now. The leaves on the trees had merged with the black sky and the air smelled pungently of the river.

"I'll think about it hard. I need to. Lately I'm starting to realize that a person who's unhappy isn't only unpleasant but a danger to their surroundings," Helena said. "But you know what? Why don't we take a walk down the embankment now, and you can tell me some of your animal stories. Maybe it will help me feel a little more human. And nothing sad or educational, please. It really has been a lovely day."

8

~

"GOOD EVENING, MRS. Kouřimská," said a tall, slim man in a beige suit, grinning wide. His hair was flecked with gray, his bony face was tanned brown, and he wore a gaudy tie bearing a family crest.

Mrs. Kouřimská beamed back. "Why, Mr. Hrůza, what a coincidence! We haven't seen each other in ages. How have you been?"

"Not bad. How about yourself? Since when are you in the movies?"

"Not long. It's only been six months since I embarked on my staggering career," Mrs. Kouřimská replied coquettishly.

"So how do you like it?"

"Oh, it's all right. But I don't come to work for fun. A job's a job. The main thing is to kill some time. But tell me, what have you been up to all these years?"

Ládinka nudged Helena with her elbow and pointed her double chin down the aisle. "Get a load of Marilyn Kouřimská flutterin' over that hunk of man. I'm tellin' you, she puts us all to shame."

"I've had a feeling about her since day one," Marie chimed in.

"What do you mean?"

"It's just . . . how can I put it? Like she's a sex fiend, but not your everyday average one. I don't know. There's somethin' funny about her."

Ládinka dashed off to the other side of the house. The movie was starting in just a few minutes and ticketholders were streaming through every door, the gaps in the rows of faces rapidly filling in. A second before the lights went down, the auditorium floor had condensed into a solid geometric plane. It was a sold-out show. One by one the ushers made their way out to the lobby.

"Hey, Mrs. Kouřimská, where'd you bag that hulk? You can tell us," said Marie.

"I should have known you'd notice, Marie," Kouřimská snapped haughtily. Clearly she was pleased

to attract the younger women's envy and couldn't resist
raising the stakes. She looked around to make sure all
the other ushers were in earshot. "In fact, not only is
he a looker," she said importantly, "he's also a man it
pays to know."

"Oh, I don't doubt you there," said Marie. "A fella
like that must come in real handy, especially if you're
in tight with him."

"Well, I didn't mean it like that," said Mrs.
Kouřimská. "You may not believe it, Marie, but most
people live, at least occasionally, outside of bed as well.
And this gentleman happens to be a big shot at the
ministry. He's got his fingers in every pie. I happen to
know because I have a friend whose fabric shop ran a
huge loss, and if it hadn't been for Mr. Hrůza she probably would have gotten ten years."

"So what did this friend of yours do for her?" Helena
asked.

"There's always a way to deal with these things. Naturally nobody discusses them in public. All I know is
he was a good friend of hers, and when she turned to
him for help, he got the whole thing kicked under the
rug. She paid a fine and that was it. Don't ask me how
he did it. I just know my friend says he's got his fingers
in every pie and no one ever tells him no."

"God forbid!" said Marie. "I'd never say no to him

either, even if he wasn't at the ministry." She slapped
a fistful of change down on the concession counter.
"Líba, fork over a box of those bonbons," she said.
"The little one."

Mrs. Kouřimská slowly made her way back to the
cloakroom. Helena stood clenching the flashlight in
her pocket.

"Mrs. Kouřimská, please, wait a minute," Helena
said, chasing her down as she opened the door to the
cloakroom.

"Yes, what is it?" Mrs. Kouřimská asked, turning
around.

"Could I talk to you for a moment?"

"Why, of course. What can I do for you?"

"Would you mind sitting here in the cloakroom?
The boss won't notice. She's in there with the accountant. There's something I'd like to ask you."

They went in and sat down on the hard, uncomfortable bench. Helena nervously lit up a smoke. Where
on earth to begin . . . ?

"Helena, what's wrong? Is it anything I can help
with?" Mrs. Kouřimská said warmly.

"No, thanks, there's nothing wrong. It's just—this
is embarrassing, but . . . I mean, we hardly know each
other, but I was hoping you could do me a favor and . . ."
Helena trailed off, giving her a pleading look.

"Out with it, Helena, what's going on? I'm happy to do whatever I can. I'm sure whatever it is, it's not impossible."

"Well, do you think you might introduce me to Mr. Hrůza? I mean, since you say he's got all that influence, and I—I could use some help. As you probably know, my husband . . ."

"Why, of course. It's hardly a secret. And you know what, you're right. It hadn't occurred to me before, but in your situation it could come in handy to know someone like him. Just to be clear, all I know is what I already told you. He isn't a close friend, just an acquaintance. But I can certainly introduce you."

"That would really be kind of you," Helena said. "How do you think we could set it up?"

"It shouldn't be too hard. I'll just wait for him after the show and you can stand here chatting with me. I'm sure as soon as he sees you, he'll want to get to know you. He's got an eye for attractive women."

"I hope you understand, Mrs. Kouřimská. I'm not Marie. That's not what I'm after. I just want to help my husband."

"I know that, Helena. But I have to warn you: Even a chicken doesn't scratch for free. I'm not telling you anything new, am I?"

Helena looked at her, dumbfounded.

"Helena," Mrs. Kouřimská said. She squinted, as if in pain.

I wonder what's so special about her that even Marie noticed, Helena thought. *Maybe it's because she spends so much time alone. I know my way around loneliness better than anyone, though. How come I didn't notice?*

The two women sat quietly a while, each absorbed in her own thoughts. Finally Mrs. Kouřimská said, "Look, this is something you have to decide for yourself. It's none of my business. But let me at least offer you this old piece of advice: Either you want something, really want it, and go for it with all your heart, no matter what the odds, and you stand at least a fighting chance of getting it. Or you only want it as long as you're not going to mess up your hair along the way, in which case you might as well spare yourself the trouble. It's like a general who wants to win a war without firing a shot."

Helena sighed. "That's just it. I still can't bring myself to look at life as a permanent war. I'd like to at least be at peace with myself. But I realize I'm just being childish. You're absolutely right, and it's kind of you to be so frank with me. The truth is I'm just not that smart and I'm not sure if I have the guts. But at least now I know what my options are. And I'd really be grateful if you could introduce me to Mr. Hrůza."

What had she been thinking, making such a drama out of it? In any case it wouldn't hurt to meet Mrs. Kouřimská's friend, and after that, the rest would depend on how she finessed it. If she could convince Hrůza that Karel really was innocent, maybe he'd be able to do something for him. It was the opportunity she'd been waiting for, and she couldn't afford to pass it up.

EVERYTHING WENT ACCORDING to script. After the show, Mrs. Kouřimská and I stood around the lobby inconspicuously and when Hrůza came out, Mrs. Kouřimská grabbed hold of him and the three of us spent a few minutes in casual conversation. Right from the start he struck me as easy to get along with. The very next day he rang me up at work and politely asked me out on a date. Taken aback by how fast he moved, I began to stutter, but he didn't miss a beat, and before I knew it I had agreed to get together that Sunday night, which I happened to have off.

Hrůza said he would wait for me in his car on the embankment. I was so nervous when I left home that I decided to cut across Žofín, where I sat on a bench and smoked two cigarettes in a row to calm myself down.

Meanwhile in my mind I had a chat with Božena Němcová, another woman who didn't exactly have it easy in life. She'd had to go through all sorts of twists and turns. And look at what a nice statue they'd made of her. I was late as a result, but Hrůza just laughed it off. It didn't bother him a bit. In general I was stunned at how civilized he was, how courteously he behaved. Up until now, I had assumed men like him went extinct in 1900. I was expecting a real lout, a slickly disguised Mephistopheles who extorted favors from desperate women. It threw me for a loop, actually. The whole ride out to Barrandov I felt uncomfortable, but then I remembered how desperate I had been for something to happen. Now finally it was and I had to handle it. Just take it slow, a move at a time. Be brave and not lose my nerve.

Hrůza was older than Karel, just the right amount of gray at the temples, suntanned and fit—in short, he looked fabulous, almost too much so. Luckily my one fancy dress still maintained a touch of flair in spite of its age. *Good old faithful*, I thought. *You're going to need a trip to the cleaners soon if you're going to last.*

It was packed at Barrandov Terraces, but Hrůza had a table reserved, naturally. An orchestra creaked out the usual assortment of light classical and operetta pieces that serve as accompaniment to good food, producing a gentle hypnotic effect on the feasting crowds. At first it seemed as if all the forks, knives, and jaws were moving in time to the melody. But as we made our way down the aisle between the tables, a head or two rose from their plates, turning to look, and some of the utensils fell out of step.

I wondered if he noticed—but how could he not, I said to myself, my mood lifting by one ever so slight but noticeable notch.

I settled into my chair as picturesquely as possible and gazed out over the railing at the river and the candlestick trunks of the black poplars beyond. How many times had I sat in this same spot with Karel—I quickly turned and smiled at the man sitting across from me now, and could tell he knew exactly what was going on with me. I hadn't even mentioned Karel yet, but all of a sudden I felt like he was sitting there at the table with us, patiently waiting his turn to talk. It took an hour and a half and three glasses of wine before I got up the courage to mention my husband. I expected it to be excruciatingly difficult, requiring the most delicate language in order not to insult Hrůza or make him angry, but as it turned out, I was completely off the mark. Bathed in sweat, I had barely stammered out the first few words when Hrůza himself started asking me questions, and the next thing I knew I had spilled the beans—not only what I wanted from him, but our whole life story, Karel's and mine, all my worries, hopes, and problems, it was like a dam had burst. At one point I suddenly stopped, wondering how I could sit there telling this absolute stranger my innermost thoughts. I began to stutter and apologize again, but Hrůza just smiled soothingly and reassured me he was interested in everything I had to say, and the way he said it I believed him.

I went on talking long after it had gotten dark. It was a magical night of opening caves and springs gushing from rocks. Never before in my life had I felt I could trust someone so fully, rely on him so completely. The protective shell I had built up over the past few months had suddenly cracked open and I felt free again. Life began to move forward, gathering speed.

By ten o'clock, Hrůza knew all there was to know about Karel, every detail I could bring myself to remember. Hrůza himself spoke very little, but what he said sounded solid: no promises or hints of connections on high. "I'll do what I can," was all he said, but that was enough for me. I knew he meant it honestly.

Afterwards, as we wound our way down the serpentine, through the black trees and back toward the city, Hrůza said it was still early, how about a glass of wine, we hadn't had that much to drink. But no sooner had we sat down at our cozy candlelit table for two and the waiter filled our glasses than he said: "Forget it. Let's go. I want to kiss you. Right now," and tossed some cash on the table.

We found ourselves back outside, under a huge summer moon so bright it outshone the streetlamps, wandering a city surreal as a dream, kissing in deserted streets, in the middle of intersections, on bridges and squares, not a soul around but us, the sole characters in some fantastical black-and-white romance.

When Hrůza unlocked the door to a beautiful old building in a lane that ran perpendicular to the river, suddenly the night turned cold and I felt a chill run through me. But then a big tabby cat came padding up to me, rubbing its head and warm bushy spine against my ankle with a meow. Sometimes Marie slept with guys and didn't even know their name. He opened the door to the entryway, but didn't switch on the light. At least I knew his name. As I stepped over the threshold I said to myself: Vojta, Vojta Hrůza.

The living room window was wide open, letting in the cold air, and I could see the silvery trees lining the embankment. Vojta turned on the radio, the green eye glowing from the console like a cat's. It was almost midnight and they were ending the broadcast for the night. As he placed his hand on the back of my neck to unzip my dress, the national anthem began to play.

Monday morning was the kind of morning that seemed inevitable after such a magical night. Barely had the day begun than I was back in the park on Žofín. Not for long. I couldn't stand the peace and quiet; the dew-covered grass, the fat, self-satisfied pigeons, and the smell of the river turned my stomach.

As the sun crept out, an elderly pensioner appeared in a blue cotton-sheen jacket probably inherited from his father. He shuffled up to the bench next to me, spread the morning paper across the damp boards, sat down, folded his hands over the handle of his cane, and peered over the top of his glasses at the blossoming chestnuts, molting sadly onto the lawn. Soon another grandfatherly type appeared at the other end of the path, identical to the first, except without a newspaper. One copy of the broadsheet more than sufficed for their two skinny bottoms. The retiree on the bench cheerfully lifted his cane in greeting.

I stood up and went back to the streets, to the lonely bustle and din, the restlessness and anxiety: that was the air I knew how to breathe.

Karel was locked up with common criminals and

murderers, and here I was whoring around with a man
I'd never even met until the day before yesterday. But
what if he really could help Karel? Wouldn't that make
it worth it? After all, was it more important for me to
sit around protecting my reputation like a saint, or for
Karel to get through his sentence as soon as he could and
come home? If I wanted to help him—and God only
knew what he must be going through every day—what
was I supposed to do? I didn't have any choice, this was
the only way. Maybe it wasn't such a bad thing, maybe
it would even bring me closer to Karel if we both sank
into the muck together, each in our own way. Once he
came back, we could put it all behind us and forget it
ever happened, but at least I'd know I wasn't too proud
to do what I could. Maybe there was once a time when
everything was clear and unambiguous and a person
could go through life without ever having to step in
shit. And if you didn't like the way the world worked,
you could just go off in a corner and sulk. But that was
over now. There was nowhere to hide. The world had
moved into our flat and brought all the muck and crap
along with it, and it didn't matter what we thought or
felt, the only question was whether we knew how to
fight back.

   I wasn't betraying Karel. It would only be a betrayal
if he didn't matter to me anymore, if I stopped caring

what happened to him. I had a chance to help him and I couldn't back out of it now. I just hoped it wasn't in vain. If Vojta had as much influence as I thought he did and he could make things better for Karel, I wouldn't regret a single minute of it.

I barely managed to crawl into work. My head was pounding and I looked like I'd been tortured, which of course didn't escape the attention of my colleagues, especially Marie. Luckily we were showing a popular comedy, so all of the screenings were crowded and my shift was practically over before I knew it.

I walked home, dawdling as much as I could, but it was no use. As soon as I unlocked the door to my flat, I could hear the phone ringing.

Two weeks later, I received a letter from Karel:

You can't even imagine, my dearest, my love, how much everything has changed for me in the past few days. Now at last I can confess how utterly dejected and hopeless I've been at times, and the only thing that has always managed to shake me out of it is the thought of you and the endless beauty of the times we've spent together. When I think of how many times I told you I loved you

without being fully aware of what I was saying.
Only during these awful months have I come to
realize that my entire life is wrapped up in our
love. Everything else is extraneous and incidental.
As long as you love me, nothing is lost forever.
We'll be together again, my darling. We just have
to hold on.

Now listen: I've been getting the papers for four
days now, I've got permission to borrow books from
the local library, and they even promised to get me
some scholarly literature and a typewriter so I can
continue my work—which is fantastic, although I
realize I can hardly produce anything under these
conditions. The main thing, however, is that my
situation is clearly taking a turn for the better and
I can have hope again, so don't worry, my love! Be
well and be patient. I'm counting on you.

It was the first real letter I had received from Karel.
All of the ones before it had read as if they'd been
copied from a template: cold and impersonal, not a
word about what he was thinking or what was going
on with him. They weren't letters so much as monthly
reports that he was still alive. Even the fact that he had
been allowed to write such a letter proved that Vojta
had had an impact, and a substantial one at that.

I spent a while carrying on like a madwoman, cheering and crying for joy. I even managed to dig an old bottle of slivovice out of the cupboard with a few drops left at the bottom and downed them in celebration of my first piece of good news, my first happy moment after months of misery, and who knew, maybe the first sign our godawful luck had finally broken.

As soon as I had recovered a bit, I gave Vojta a call and thanked him in the silkiest voice that I could muster. Of course he denied any credit for it, and I understood. It wasn't just his natural modesty and refined moral sense. One simply didn't discuss such matters. He couldn't explain anything and in fact there was no need. It was clear from my husband's letter that Vojta was serious in his intention to help, and above all that he was actually capable of doing so. I didn't want to get my hopes up. Nothing in this world was certain. But, on the other hand, anything was possible.

I agreed to meet Vojta that night after I got out of work. Lately we had been seeing each other pretty often, and even though I still had bouts of deep depression, on the whole our relationship had stabilized surprisingly quickly. Vojta knew I was only going out with him because of Karel; I knew that he knew; and we both knew that the whole thing was only temporary. And yet, something strange happened:

From the moment we met, Vojta was so closely connected to Karel for me that he soon started to seem
like Karel's stand-in, like someone Karel himself had
sent me to take his place—almost like his double,
his other self. And since Vojta didn't expect me to
pretend anything or lie to him, some of the initial
tension had faded away and I was beginning to feel
more relaxed around him.

So maybe I had done the right thing after all. Karel's
situation had improved so much, and I—well, at least
I wasn't on my own all the time anymore . . .

9

THE DOOR KNOCKER clinked three times.

The woman got up and quickly crossed the bedroom to the entryway. Her body was cold all over and her hands twitched like there was an electric current running through them.

I'm going to get a shock when I touch the door handle, she thought.

Two girls stood in the doorway. Renata, sixteen, held the hand of Zdenka, three years her junior. The older girl smiled gently.

"Karla, this is Zdenka. The one you wanted to meet."

"Please, come in," said the woman.

The younger girl stepped over the threshold and stood in the entryway.

"Renata, why don't you take Zdenka into the living room and I'll bring you two a treat."

The woman went into the kitchen and picked up a tray she had prepared with glasses and open-faced sandwiches. Renata slipped in behind her and closed the door.

"I told her two hundred. Are we good?" she asked.

"That's fine. But where's little Vera? I thought she was—"

"She can't come. Her parents made up and now they're home every night, so she can't get out. She isn't happy about it either. She liked you, and the money came in handy."

"What a shame. Isn't there anything you can do?"

"Well, only if her mom and dad start fighting again—there's always a chance. But doesn't look like it for now."

She took the tray out of the woman's hand and put it back on the table next to a dish of cake and chocolates.

"Look, Karla, you know I'd walk through fire for you. I don't do this for money. But it's not exactly easy rounding up girls and organizing all this. So do you mind if we settle up first? Three hundred for me and two for Zdenka, like we agreed."

The woman opened the table drawer, took out a sealed envelope, and handed it to Renata. The girl tore it open and laid the bills on the table, riffling through them like a veteran cashier.

"Great. Thanks a mil." The reflection of the money disappeared from her eyes, but she lingered another moment out of conscientiousness. "You can count on me, you know. If one can't make it, there's always another."

"I really thought little Vera was . . ."

Renata stuck the envelope in her jeans' back pocket and smiled. The pink cheeks on her round, chubby face grew even rounder.

"Look, Zdenka might be even better. And it doesn't look like her folks'll be making up anytime soon. She's free whenever—we just have to call. This could be a lasting relationship. You always said that's what you wanted, right? Course you got one with me, but I'm gettin' too old for you, aren't I? You like 'em young, I know you! But you don't stand a chance without me, honey. What would you do without me, huh?"

She reached for the sash on the woman's pink brocade robe.

The woman shrank back.

"Wait, we don't want to frighten the little one!"

"Don't worry, sweetheart. She knows why she's here.

I explained everything. She may be young and stupid, but she's eager to learn. She can hardly wait."

Renata picked up the dish of cake and walked out of the kitchen.

The woman in the pink robe stood stiffly holding the tray. The expression on her face was calm, almost stern.

That filthy slut. It's terrible, it's awful. I'd like to boot her right out the window. And jump out after her. God, my God, have mercy, help me, give me the strength not to do this. I've given up everything else as I've gotten older, but it seems like there's no end to this.

The woman stood not moving, almost not breathing, waiting for the wave of disgust and hatred to pass. A gaping emptiness slowly spread through her head. The pulse in her neck throbbed. She could feel herself tremble as the blood rushed through her veins.

I'm the wind, the waves, the flood. I sweep away whatever I touch.

She opened the door to the living room. The glasses clinked thinly on the tray. The teenaged Zdenka squeezed the chair's armrests with both hands and lifted her head.

10

~

THIS TIME THE man tossed the yellow envelope onto the table before he picked up the glass of beer the woman had poured for him. He looked tired and grouchy. The woman watched him tensely, waiting for him to speak. The man pointed to the envelope: "Go ahead, you earned it, even if it didn't all go quite the way we planned."

"What do you mean, I—"

"Oh, it's not your fault. Sometimes things just don't work out, not much you can do. Lot of risks in this line of work. All kinds."

"So tell me, what happened? I'm knee-deep in it too, after all. At least I should know what I'm doing."

"Actually it's none of your business. That's not our arrangement, that I'm the one who reports to you, but just for your information, Šípek is probably our man. We gave him a little going-over, just a preliminary thing. He's holdin' out of course—as you'd expect— but it looks promising. And it makes sense. Knows all sorts of languages, subscribes to foreign journals—hey, these zoologists, it's an international field. You got guys comin' in from the West all the time. Just recently there was some congress and Šípek was showin' people around, socializing and whatnot. Ideally placed for espionage. We need to put him through the wringer. So my compliments, you did a great job, and to show our appreciation your envelope's fatter today. Bonus."

The woman pinched her lips but said nothing.

The man raised his empty glass. The woman stood up, went to the kitchen, and brought a new bottle back from the fridge.

"So all this'd be fine." The man opened the bottle, poured the beer into the glass, and waited, bottle in hand, for the foam to settle. He filled the glass the rest of the way and set the bottle down on the table.

"Except. The other thing didn't work out like it

was supposed to, goddam job. It isn't your fault Hrůza screwed up. He questioned Novák for months. Zilch, not a thing. So he figured he'd try a sneak attack. Guy in jail like that, his doll back home's all he can think of. Or the kids, depending. Even the toughest egg'll soften up when he finds out his ladylove has thrown him to the wolves. And that's what Hrůza was counting on."

The man paused, resting his elbows on his knees, and leaned forward, head down. He was quiet so long the woman was afraid he had fallen asleep. Finally he sat back upright.

"Yeah, so as you know, he worked on Helena Nováková a bit, then took her to a hotel one weekend. When she fell asleep, he took some pictures. Real artworks. First just her, then the two of 'em together in bed, with a timer. Gorgeous shots. Guy's a real pro, yep. Then he showed 'em to Novák."

The man cleared his throat and reached for his glass. The woman clasped her hands in her lap.

"Only then, instead of cavin' in like most guys would, the jerk went completely off the deep end. Just blew a fuse. Started actin' all crazy, sayin' he was going to kill Hrůza with his bare hands. Then when they took him back to his cell, he tore up his grays, made a noose, and hanged himself from his cell window bars. I just found out. Goddam mess."

He heaved a deep sigh and curled up in the arm-chair, staring blankly into space. After a while he rose heavily to his feet, shrugged, and threw out his hands.

"Now Hrůza's been runnin' around with her a month. All that time, all that money, and the whole thing's down the drain. Anyway, like I said, Karla, no one can blame you for it."

Still standing, he threw back the rest of his beer, turned and, as always, marched out of the room without a good bye, slamming the door behind him.

Mrs. Kouřimská stiffly rose to her feet and walked to the window. The man stepped out onto the street. In the light of the streetlamp his thick hair, cropped short, glittered like purest silver.

11

~

THE HORIZON WAS playing an English detective film. It was sold out every day, with long lines at the box office. The ushers had their work cut out for them. The days were hot and muggy, and even late at night it didn't cool down much. People roamed along the river all night long, till their hair was damp with dew. Life sagged and slowed with the heat.

Marie walked out of the cinema and trudged wearily down the street. *As soon as this is all over, I'm putting in for some sick days*, she thought. The last six months had been just too much. She was barely dragging her feet.

On the wall above the stairs leading down to the

river, adorned with graffiti and doodles, a new demonstration of folk creativity had appeared: a beautifully shaped heart—only inside it, instead of the usual initials, were the numbers 15–3. Marie stopped a moment, then slowly made her way down the stairs.

As soon as she got in the elevator, she began to unbutton her dress, and the moment she stepped through the door of her flat, she flung her handbag onto the chair and headed straight to the bathroom to run herself a cold bath. Then she stretched out on the daybed, too big for only one, and listened to the water streaming from the faucet. *I'm not even going to eat anything, just take a bath and hit the hay. Then after a couple days' rest, I'll start looking around for some nice, ordinary guy I can love in a nice, ordinary way, like normal people do.*

A large gray moth flew in the open window and circled around the lamp. Disgusted, Marie switched off the light and hopped into the tub in the dark.

The next day before leaving for work, Marie rummaged through the cookie tin that served as her medicine cabinet until she found a smudged envelope that said BAND-AIDS in blue and red letters. She pulled out a large square adhesive bandage and, using her nail, peeled back a corner of the gauze pad. Underneath was a black dot the size of a pinhead. She didn't look any further. She knew all she would find was a few more exactly identical dots. She pressed the pad back against the adhesive, pulled up her skirt, and attached the bandage to her upper thigh. She tossed the envelope with the blue and red writing into her handbag, stepped up to the mirror, ran a comb through her hair, and made a face at herself.

"And away we go," she said out loud.

The show was of course sold out again, and the house was nearly full by the time the lights went down. Five minutes in, Marie went out to the hallway and slipped through the door marked LADIES. She had the whole place to herself. Hissing softly, she peeled the bandage away from her skin. She took the blue-and-red envelope from the pocket of her work smock, inserted the bandage, resealed the envelope, and placed it back in her pocket. Then she returned to the auditorium and leaned against the wall next to the middle door. Exactly ten minutes after the start of the screening, a chubby, bespectacled man of middle age burst through the door. He was clearly upset to be late, as evidenced by the fact that he was gasping for breath from his rush to get there. Marie took his ticket and flashed her light on it. Row fifteen, seat three. She led the portly gentleman down the aisle to his row, and he squeezed past the other grumpily

muttering viewers to his seat. As he settled in, he stole
a glance at his neighbor to the right: a boy of about
fourteen, eyes glued to the screen. The fat man reached
into his right-hand jacket pocket, finding a small
crumpled envelope with his fingertips. As slowly and
inconspicuously as possible, he withdrew the envelope
and dropped it to the floor. Then he rested his shoe
on top of it, so he could kick it away if needed. Only
then did he make himself comfortable and devote his
undivided attention to the film.

Three minutes before the end, the portly man
removed his glasses—apparently they had clouded
up—and began fumbling for his handkerchief. He
succeeded in cleaning them, but managed to drop
his handkerchief on the floor in the process. Groping
around in the dark a while, he finally found it and
folded it neatly back into his pocket. The lights in the
house went up and the audience began to rise from
their seats. The fat man docilely shuffled out with the
rest of them, and on reaching the street, he breathed in
the hot, thick, dust-choked evening air with a smile of
delight.

The cinema emptied out unusually slowly. Even the
ushers weren't in a rush to get home. Helena, Marie,
and Mrs. Kouřimská climbed the staircase together and
plodded out through the lobby. Mrs. Kouřimská barely

nodded good-bye and took the first right down toward the embankment. Helena and Marie stopped and stared after her.

"Have you noticed?" asked Helena.

"How could I not," answered Marie. "Even the boss has been asking if we know what's goin' on with her. Ládinka says she just hopes it isn't cancer."

"I don't think so. I'd say more like she's in a jam. She seems more troubled than sick."

"And what a woman she was just a few days ago. I always thought she'd get old slow, but it's like all the years just suddenly piled up on top of her."

"Maybe it's the heat. It's getting to me too."

"It's gettin' to everyone. Everyone's actin' funny. And there's some funny things going on. Yesterday I heard the Podolí pool was crammed like a barrel of carp before Christmas, and at night when they let out the water they found a dead guy at the bottom. Drowned right in the middle of all those people, jumpin' and splashin' and horsin' around. Nobody even noticed."

They were still standing in front of the cinema. Helena looked up and down the street.

"It's been a few days since that pretty boy of yours put in an appearance, huh?" said Marie. "Can't say I'm surprised. Probably lyin' at home in the bath. I don't know any love strong enough to make a guy climb out of the tub on a scorcher like this."

"I don't know what's going on with him," Helena said anxiously. It had been three days now since Vojta had shown his face, or even called. She thought back to their last date, but couldn't recall anything to suggest an impending breakup. *We had a good time*, she thought. *Something must've happened. Maybe one of those "funny" things.* Suddenly, out of nowhere, a high, thin note, a silver chord of fear, twanged in her head. And it slowly began getting louder.

She nearly grabbed Marie by the hand. *Oh God, don't let her leave yet*, she thought, in a state of near-panic.

"And what about your captain?" Helena quickly asked.

"Aw, that's gone and died on the vine. It was startin' to look like we might get permanently hitched, and you know me, I'm not cut out for marital bliss. Assumin' there even is such a thing. Can't say as I've ever seen it. Anyways, look at all the guys waltzin' down the street and here we are traipsin' home alone. Though, truth is, I wouldn't mind so much bein' by myself if . . ."

" . . . if you weren't alone. I know what you mean. There's alone, more alone, and most alone of all."

"Exactly," said Marie. "When you know there's somebody out there, even if they're all the way on the other side of the world, you might be alone, but you don't feel it so much. You got an advantage over me when it comes to that."

The noise in Helena's head began to chatter so loudly it drowned out everything else, sending tremors all the way out to her fingertips.

"Bye now," said Marie, turning to walk away, but Helena gave no reply. She just stood there, engulfed in herself and the horror eating its way into her like a ravine carving itself into the surface of the earth. Finally she managed to snap out of it and dashed off down the street, running all the way home, mailbox key clenched in her hand. Breathlessly she burst in the door and unlocked the tall shiny box to find her fears confirmed: a long white envelope with an official letterhead in the left-hand corner.

PART II

1

THE WHOLE RIGHT-HAND side of the building that housed the Horizon was taken up by the glass wall of the Black Cat snack bar, like an aquarium set into the facade. From her post behind the counter, Božena Šulcová commanded a view of the entire lobby of the Horizon, as well as both directions up and down Broad Street, and to her right, around the corner, a short lane just one block long, aptly named Steep Street.

It was already after 10 P.M. On any other day Božena would have been getting ready to close, but today it was the last thing on her mind. She pressed her body against the glass to the right of the counter, trying to see as far as she could down Steep Street.

"Don't waste your time," said the last customer of the day, a fatherly old man in a tram driver's uniform, wiping the last dab of mustard from his plate with the tip of his frankfurter. "Can't see a thing from here. Must've happened down the far end of the street. Officers ain't lettin' anyone in. Say there's a body down there."

"Body?" Božena said excitedly. "Some sorta traffic accident?"

"Naw. But could be someone got run over."

"I'll find out one way or another," Božena said, catching the eye of one of the men in uniform out on the sidewalk. She tipped her head and the officer grinned and winked. He was a familiar face. Came to the snack bar almost every day for a black brawn and beer. *He'll be in soon enough*, Božena thought to herself, satisfied, going back behind the counter.

"That'll be six fifty," she said. The tram driver laid the change down on a small rubber mat, put on his cap, and stood up.

"They can't get anything by you, Božena, love. I've no worries there," he said as he walked to the door.

Božena picked up a rag and began wiping down the counter, but she didn't take her eyes off the street outside for a second. To her left, moviegoers were coming out of the cinema. To her right, in the middle of the street, a traffic policeman stood preventing vehicles from turning into Steep Street and directing them to continue down Broad Street instead. Shiny black cars barricaded Steep Street at both ends, with officers in uniform winding in and out. A little further on, past the point where Božena could see from her post, an old dark-blue Škoda was parked, with a cluster of men in civilian dress standing beside it. One, a pudgy, pink-cheeked blond, was diligently taking down notes in a thick black notepad. Leaning against the hood of the car, a muscular, dark-haired man with sparkling-black gypsy eyes examined the driver, who was sitting behind the wheel but tipped over so far to the side that his head rested against the car window. On the seat next to him was a young man in a white coat with a stethoscope around his neck and a hardened look on his face. It was his first police case and he was doing his best to give the impression of a seasoned veteran, his face showing nothing even as his stomach lurched uncomfortably. He pointed to the handle of the knife protruding from the chest of the man behind the wheel, cleared his throat, and said in a voice distinctly higher than usual:

"There's nothing else here to investigate. The knife penetrated the heart, resulting in immediate death. He didn't put up a struggle. In fact he appeared to take it rather calmly." The doctor touched his fingertips to the eyelids of the deceased.

"It's possible he was dozing. From the looks of it, I'd say it happened around eight o'clock. Give or take."

"Did it take a lot of strength?" the dark-eyed bruiser asked.

The young doctor ran two fingers along the dead man's chest.

"Not really," he said. "The knife went between the ribs. Perfect aim. Could be knowledge of anatomy, or could be sheer coincidence. That's about all I can say for now. To be continued after the autopsy."

The doctor opened the car door and stepped out.

The brown-skinned policeman turned to the fat blond. "Comrade Koloušek, make sure everything follows proper procedure. Report back to me in an hour for further instructions."

"Yes sir, Comrade Lieutenant," the butterball said eagerly.

The lieutenant made his way through the clump of vehicles on Broad Street. When he reached the corner, he stopped and glanced across the street. A tall, thin man with graying temples stood staring down Steep Street over the heads of the gawkers. *Wait, isn't that . . . ?* Before the lieutenant could finish his thought, the man slowly turned and walked off, down Broad, toward the embankment. The lieutenant followed him with his eyes a while, then climbed into one of the black automobiles, and the driver pulled away. The lieutenant didn't need to name his destination.

The white lace hem of a nightgown peeked out from under the woman's dark-blue robe. It was surprisingly unseductive. Mrs. Nedomová dabbed at her red eyes and nose with a large handkerchief as she paced back and forth across the room. Lieutenant Vendyš sat hunched on the edge of his chair, watching unhappily. This was the worst part of his profession. At this point, looking at dead bodies, no matter how mutilated they were, was just part of the job and he didn't let his imagination get the better of him. He kept his emotions out of his investigations, too. But the first conversation with the victim's closest relatives was always a challenge for him and he rarely handled it well. Usually it was all he could do to rattle off a few sentences, informing them of the basic facts in as condensed a form as possible, then remove himself to the corner and sit with his mouth shut, desperately awaiting a chance to get out with his honor intact.

Lieutenant Vendyš, along with the rest of his

colleagues, had been required by the ministry to undergo a two-week training course in psychology. Yet for deep-seated psychological reasons he categorically rejected the idea that the subject was of any use in his profession. His line of work was human acts—more to the point, criminal acts—which was problematic enough as it was. Where would he end up if on top of all that he had to poke around in people's heads?

The only situations where he admitted the training might come in handy were ones like this, where a little knowledge of the human soul, so to speak, could be useful. How do you break the news to someone that their loved one has met with a violent death—telling them in the least painful way possible, and even more important, causing the least amount of uproar? There probably was no way. Some things just had to run their course. Sometimes with surprising results. Like with Mrs. Nedomová here. The lieutenant hadn't expected her to take it so hard. Nedoma had hardly been a model husband, and everybody knew it.

"I'm sure you know as well as anyone that Václav wasn't exactly a model husband," Mrs. Nedomová told the lieutenant. "I myself am surprised I'm so upset. I've wanted a divorce for ages now. But still, it's not the same."

She sniffled and raised the handkerchief to her eyes. It was damp, but not that damp.

Vendyš muttered something unintelligible. Of course it wasn't the same, he thought. Just because you wanted to end a failed marriage didn't mean you wanted the other person dead. Although—once things got to the point where a husband and wife couldn't live together anymore, it must be a lot easier, and more respectable, to be widowed than divorced. Especially for a woman. Death had a way of erasing the abuse, balancing out the humiliation. It was easy to forgive a dead man: *After all, it wasn't his choice to leave me, poor guy. Maybe there was still a chance we could have gotten back together. He used to be so in love with me . . . I need to be able to stand up and take the blow.* On the other hand, getting a divorce meant admitting to the entire world—including your children and yourself—that your marriage was bankrupt and you couldn't make it work. You didn't know how to keep a husband or a home . . . Divorce was always so awkward and unpleasant, and it could drag on and on, whereas . . .

Vendyš unconsciously registered the muscular forearm poking out of the sleeve of Mrs. Nedomová's robe. "We called you as soon as . . ." His voice trailed off into an embarrassed cough. "But there was no answer. So I came right over."

"Yes, I just got in a half hour ago. I was out," Mrs. Nedomová said vaguely. Vendyš shot her a questioning look, but didn't dare probe any further just yet.

Mrs. Nedomová started pacing around the room again. "What will I tell the girls? How do you tell your children they don't have a father anymore?"

She came to a stop in the middle of the room, thought for a moment, then vigorously blew her nose and wiped her eyes. She tucked the handkerchief into her robe pocket and turned to the lieutenant.

"Thank you, Comrade Vendyš. I know you have your hands full. You did what you could. From here on in I'll have to fend for myself. And forgive me for being so agitated."

The lieutenant cleared his throat again. "Oh, don't worry. I wish I could do more to help. It's such a terrible thing to have happen . . . If there's anything you need, of course . . . Before I go, there's just one thing I'd like to ask, if you don't mind . . ."

Mrs. Nedomová nodded.

"Well, I was wondering if you have any idea what the captain might have been doing on Steep Street? Who or what he was waiting for? Maybe there was some . . . private reason he was there. As far as we know, he wasn't working a case in the area. But of course we're just getting our investigation going . . ."

Mrs. Nedomová looked hesitant at first, then sighed. "Well, I can tell you this, even though I might be better off keeping it to myself. Steep Street's next door to the Horizon, right? At one point Václav had a case there, which I'm sure you're aware of, and then he had a lady friend there, which you may not be aware of. But as far as I know, he broke it off with her quite painlessly some time ago. That's all I know. Václav never confided in me about anything, and I never asked."

The lieutenant remained sitting a little while longer on the edge of his seat, studying the red-and-black pattern of the carpet. Then he rose, offered his hand to the widowed woman, and choked out a few more words of condolence.

"I'll be back in touch tomorrow, and if there's anything at all you need . . ."

Mrs. Nedomová escorted the lieutenant to the door, locked it behind him, and went back to the living room. She sat down in the armchair and broke down in anguished sobs, holding nothing back. She cried and cried—you might even say she put her heart into it. It was more an outburst of relief than of despair, but there was also a wistfulness to it, since perverse beings that we are, we always regret what we've lost, even if it was just suffering.

Finally she got up, went to the bathroom, and gave her face a thorough scrubbing in cold water.

"There, you see, Václav?" she said to the mirror, rubbing her face with a towel. "I cried so many tears over you when you were alive. It's almost a pleasure now to cry because you're dead. Here's hoping I won't have a reason to cry anymore."

She returned to the living room and stood a moment, thinking, then went to the phone and dialed a number. It rang several times before someone picked up.

"Hello," she said as a wary voice answered quietly on the other end. "Hello, Nedomová here. Is that you, Miss Vránová?"

2

⁓

Božena pushed through the heavy glass door and set her bulging striped canvas bag on the ground. She took a pouch of keys from her pocket, pulled the door to by its vertical handle, wrestled the key into the lock, and gave it a turn. Then, tugging the handle once to make sure it was locked, she picked up her bag and stepped onto the sidewalk. Stopping to take in a view of the crowd of gawkers at the corner of Steep Street, she spotted Ládinka coming out of the lobby with Líba and waited for them to join her.

"Hey, Božena. What's all the fuss about?" Ládinka asked.

"Lemme tell you, ladies," Božena began, having had

a moment or two to assemble the speech in her head.
"I am amazed! There's earth-shaking events takin'
place, right outside our door, and you ask what's goin'
on? Lucky for you you got me here to break the news
to you gently, or you'd be in for a serious shock. Now
listen up: There's a beat-up sedan parked right over
there, and sittin' inside it's a man we all know—some
of us better than others. Gorgeous silver hair, always
keeps it perfectly trimmed. Somebody took a knife to
him and stabbed the life right outta him."

Ládinka and Líba looked at each other in horror.

"Ain't it somethin', girls?" Božena chattered on. "It's
like there's a spell on this place. What doesn't happen
here? We got more drama off screen than on it."

"I wouldn't get too excited if I were you," Líba said.
"Once the men in blue get their hooks into you, you
won't know your up from your down. You've got a
front-row view from that aquarium of yours, and everybody knows it. D'you see anything out of the ordinary?"

"Well now, wouldn't you girls like to know?" Božena
laughed. She was in her element. Fat and unattractive,
with swollen legs and a head of hair that looked moth-
eaten, Božena, never wrapped in a loving embrace in
her life, or even glanced at with affection, was about
to become the center of attention. "It's like they say:
everyone gets their chance in life. Well, this is mine."

"Whatever you say, Božena. Bye now," Líba said. "C'mon, Ládinka, let's get outta here. I'll tell you one thing. I'm givin' my notice next month and you won't see me in this hole in the ground again as long as I live. Me and Petr are goin' away on a honeymoon to the Bohemian Forest, and when we get back I'm gonna find myself a normal job. This whole place is downright deranged."

"Course it is," Ládinka said, popping a bonbon into her mouth. "One, it isn't normal working only with women. And two, it's nuts bein' at work when everyone else is out tearin' up the town. Look at us. We're a bunch of freaks. All except for you."

"I told you to stop stuffin' your face with chocolate all the time, Ládinka. If you want to see what's goin' on, be my guest, but I'm gone. Murder's not my thing. I'm into life. My life. Nice, calm, happy. If other people wanna kill each other so bad, let 'em go right ahead. Hey, there's Petr now. See you tomorrow, Ládinka."

Líba waved to a young man in a red T-shirt with hair so light it was practically white, and ran off to meet him. He wrapped an arm around her shoulders.

"Hey, Šemík," Líba said. "Don't you know how to give a woman a proper pagan greeting?"

"Be thou hale, good Princess Libuše," said the long-haired young man, kissing her with a loud smack. "I mean, be hale but not so hale that you forget to call in sick one of these days. The two of us need to take a trip out of town while we're still single. It won't be as much fun once we're married and respectable. Oh, and in case you haven't heard, somebody got stabbed today next door to your work. No joke!"

"I know and I couldn't care less. I see so many murders on screen every day, it doesn't even faze me anymore. So when should I take off? Hope the weather holds up. Autumn's just around the corner." The two of them walked away, snuggled in each other's arms.

Ládinka dug another bonbon out of her pocket and peeled off the wrapper. Then she turned and shuffled back toward the cluster of people gathered on the corner. She easily elbowed her way through to the mouth of Steep Street, and everyone stepped aside so she could have a look. There was nothing to see anyway. She just caught a glimpse as two uni-forms parted to let a dark-haired, broad-shouldered man pass between them onto Broad Street. He stood a moment, gazing across the street, then climbed into one of the black sedans parked along the sidewalk. He sat down in front, next to the driver, and the car pulled away from the curb.

What a hunk, Ládinka thought, biting into her candy. *Maybe he'll come and investigate us at the Horizon.*

I mean, unless he's completely soft in the head, he'll have to come see us sooner or later.

Suddenly it dawned on her that the whole thing wasn't actually as exciting as she had thought. Maybe nothing would come of it. She turned, pushing aside a few people to make her way back toward the tram. She fumbled around in her pocket for another bonbon, but she'd already eaten the last one.

Mrs. Kouřimská climbed heavily up the stairs, passed through the lobby, and exited onto Broad Street. Two traffic policemen stood at the base of Steep Street, dispersing the crowd to make way for the ambulance, but Mrs. Kouřimská didn't even turn to look, as if nothing that happened on this earth could possibly be of interest to her. She just plowed straight ahead down the street, head down, arms pinned to her sides. *Home*, she said doggedly to herself. *I just want to be home, alone . . .*

She stopped impatiently at the corner by the embankment, standing on the edge of the curb, cars whizzing past. A second before the light turned green, a tall man in a beige suit appeared at her side. He stood so close their hands almost touched. She glanced up, then staggered back as if punched in the gut. The look of menace in the pale blue eyes between his graying temples took her breath away.

A stream of people poured into the roadway, dragging her with them. She broke into a frantic run toward the bridge, but only made it a few steps. She stumbled and caught hold of the stone balustrade, leaning against it for support, and turned to look. The man stood erect on the corner, his head towering over the other pedestrians, implacable, unmoving, staring straight at her. *He knows*, she thought, heart pounding in her throat. *He knows Nedoma told me. He knows everything . . . and he's lying in wait for me.*

Helena left the Horizon just a few minutes after Mrs. Kouřimská. She made her way down the street, teeming with people, as if she were walking alone down a tunnel. Lately she'd had the feeling that the air around her was like a thick, heavy curtain she had to draw back in order to see anything. There wasn't much that was worth the effort.

The street corner was nothing but a solid wall of backs. She paused a moment to gaze absently, only half seeing the scene, then moved on, not stopping again until she reached the bridge. She leaned over the railing, staring listlessly into the water.

Out of some animal instinct for self-preserva-
tion Helena continued to go to work and perform
her simple duties, returning home at the end of the
day, sometimes eating a meal, and occasionally even
getting an hour of sleep. Meanwhile her head swam
with shapeless fragments of thought, splintered rec-
ollections of circumstances and events, but all the
connections that normally gave them meaning kept
dropping out, like the power shutting off when a
machine is overloaded.

Almost every day, on her way home from work, she
would stop and stare down at the river, submerging
herself in its quiet, endless flow. If she looked long
enough, she began to have the feeling of being
carried along with the current, gently, soothingly
floating away from the solid permanence of the
human world, away from all those incomprehensible
and immutable things . . . further and further, never to
return, leaving behind the objects that defined her by
the fact that they belonged to her, a part of her past and
an assumption of her existence in the future . . .

The solitude separating Helena from other people
was starting to distance her from inanimate things
as well, stealing into her brain, where every thought
floated unanchored in the void, like a scrap of cloud in
a smooth summer sky.

"Helena," said a voice next to her. A large, slightly calloused palm came to rest on top of her hand. She turned and found herself staring straight at the pocket of a men's plaid shirt.

"Helena," the voice said again.

Helena slowly lifted her eyes and arched the back of her hand so it nestled against the man's palm. Mr. Šípek smiled gratefully.

"Would you like to take a stroll in the park? Or sit down somewhere for a while? It's such a lovely evening."

Helena shook her head. All of a sudden, that familiar voice, those familiar words, broke through the fog she was in. She felt the rough texture of the stone beneath her fingers; the breath of the river, tinged with the sharpness of autumn, on her cheeks. Behind her she heard people's footsteps and voices, and thought to herself in amazement: *I'm alive. I can hear, smell, breathe. I feel pain. I'm alive.* Tears gushed from her eyes, streaming down her face and splashing on the stone railing next to her hand. Neither one of them so much as stirred as she felt the pain gathering inside her like a wave, like a surge of water crashing against a cliff. The only way to withstand such an onslaught was to ride it out in stillness. The man knew it and patiently waited.

When at last they walked across the bridge toward Helena's flat, Šípek said, "If you don't mind, Helena, now I hope you'll listen to me: Today somebody murdered Captain Nedoma, the one who investigated that boy who was killed where you work. It happened on Steep Street apparently. I was milling around there, hoping I might catch sight of you, when the officers came swooping in. At this point the Horizon is the center of the web, where all points converge. They're probably going to question you, and everyone else who works there. They'll probably come down on me too. I'm sure it didn't escape their notice that I was in the area. But it isn't me I'm worried about. It's you."

Helena said quietly, "I've got one big advantage over you. There's nothing left that anyone can do to me. The worst has already happened."

Šípek looked at his hand, where the salty spray of Helena's tears had landed just moments before, and smiled sadly. Being in regular contact with nature and creatures subject to the same senseless, irredeemable suffering as humans had taught him that this sentence, like the original name of God, was best left unspoken, as it only took on meaning at the moment of our death. But all he said was:

"Did you ever run into him I mean Nedoma again after he came to the Horizon?"

Helena narrowed her eyes in concentration. Her memories of the whole thing were like cloudy water.

A muddy pond. It was work to fish anything out of it. She shook her head.

"No. Not that I recall. I'm almost sure I never saw him again. I think Marie had a thing with him. But that doesn't concern me. I don't have to tell anyone, do I?"

"I wouldn't think so. But we'll see. I'm sure she'll tell them herself. It's not the kind of thing you can keep secret. We just have to hope they don't harass you too much." He paused a moment, then said tentatively, "So what happened with that tall gray-haired man I used to see you with?"

Helena took her time answering.

"He's a friend of mine," she said slowly. "Sort of an odd situation. He wanted to help. Made a promise and did what he could. He genuinely tried. But in the end it was still no use. I'm not seeing him anymore."

Šípek took her hand and they walked a while in silence. He would have liked to ask if she had found out anything more about Karel's death, about the cause of his suicide, but didn't dare. Helena was thinking the same: *Why did you do it, Karel, why? How could you leave me that way?*

They stood a while in front of Helena's building before she went inside. As she reached the elevator and pressed her finger to the button, she turned and looked back at Šípek, standing in the doorway, just as he had the first time she saw him. Only this time he wasn't smiling.

If only he knew, Helena thought as she stepped into the elevator.

Marie was the last one to leave the Horizon. When she reached the street she stopped and watched the crowd on the corner a while. She seemed to be trying to make up her mind whether she should go and look, too. In the end she couldn't resist, heading straight for the cluster of onlookers, finding the ideal spot, standing on her tiptoes, and craning her neck to get the best view she could. Just then, a short fat man in metal-rimmed glasses bumped into her. The impact threw her off balance. She stumbled and hopped to the side. The obese man caught her by the arm. "Pardon me, excuse me, I'm so sorry," he said. Marie wrenched free of his grip, smiled mechanically, and went along her way.

She walked home, taking advantage of the time to do some thinking. She climbed to the third floor of her building and unlocked the door to her studio flat, created by walling off the kitchen, pantry, and maid's room from a former upper-class family flat. The rooms here were far more spacious than in the

new buildings, and despite the incredible mess she
so systematically cultivated, it was surprisingly cozy.
Today in particular. From the moment she set foot
inside and turned on the lights, a feeling of safety and
calm washed over her. *My refuge*, she thought. She
changed into her kaleidoscopic robe, then went to the
kitchen and brewed herself some Turkish coffee. She
swept the heap of magazines off her armchair onto
the floor, and settled in, coffee in hand. Looking
around the room, she spied a crumpled pack of cigarettes on the floor by the wall beneath the wardrobe.
She set her coffee down on the table next to the chair
and stretched her arm as far as she could, managing
to reach the packet without getting up. She pulled a
box of matches from the pocket of her robe, did her
best to straighten one of the cigarettes, which were
missing half their tobacco, and lit it. She needed to
do some hard thinking.

Just as she looked at her watch and decided she
might as well call it a night, the phone rang. Marie's
heart started pounding. *Who could that be, except . . .
I won't pick up . . . but that'll just make it worse . . . It'll
look suspicious if I'm not at home . . . Everything needs
to look totally normal . . .*

The phone rang again. Marie lifted the receiver.

"Hello?" she said softly.

"Hello," a woman's voice said. "Nedomová here. Is that you, Miss Vránová? Are you alone?"

"Yes," said Marie, still startled.

"Listen, I don't know if you've heard yet, but somebody murdered poor Václav tonight. Right next to your cinema, too. The police were just here and I alerted them to the fact that he had certain dealings at the Horizon—meaning you."

"But . . ." Marie stammered.

"I know the two of you called it quits ages ago," Mrs. Nedomová said with her usual directness. "And if it comes to that, I will testify to it under oath. But I had to tell them. I don't think it will do you any harm. On the contrary. If I had acted like I didn't know, it would have looked suspicious. After all, everyone knows I'm not stupid. And in this situation I can't afford to have the police think I'm hiding anything. The same goes for you. Do you see what I mean?"

There was a moment of silence. Then Marie said, "Thank you, I think you're right. When it comes to these things, a person should lie as little as possible. But how come you're—"

"Warning you about it?" Mrs. Nedomová said. "Well, partly because we both know what sort of man Václav was. He caused so much suffering while he was alive and no one could do a thing about it. So I think now that he's gone, it's time he left us alone." She paused a moment, then said, more to herself than Marie, "It does make me a little sad, but I swear, I can't tell if it's for him, because he's dead, or for myself, because he lived with me."

Mrs. Nedomová cleared her throat and picked back up in her usual voice. "Well, the other reason I'm calling is so you have a chance to think about what you want to say and how you want to say it. The investigator, Lieutenant Vendyš, is an honest man but he suffers from an inferiority complex. He's terrified of women and doesn't have the faintest idea how to deal with them. He just searches through the handful of pigeonholes he keeps in his head, and as long as you fit neatly into one of them, he's happy and you've won. You just have to be the simple-minded type, get it?"

"I get it," said Marie. "The type that doesn't have the brains to commit a crime."

"Exactly," said Mrs. Nedomová. "I'm glad we understand each other. Good night, then. I'll keep my fingers crossed for you."

"Good night," Marie said and hung up the phone. *But I wouldn't be so sure we understand each other*, she thought.

3

LIEUTENANT VENDYŠ INHERITED his eyes, so perfectly black you couldn't tell the pupil from the iris, from his mother, who was born in a small town in western Slovakia. To this day, when he had nightmares, it was always the same dream. He saw a rock, in slow motion, sailing in a huge arc across the blue sky, then falling, down, down, down, into the windowpane, then a shower of broken glass and his mother's wild, beautiful face emerging from it bit by bit, larger than life, two black thunderbolts shooting sparks, her muscular peasant arm gripping a bamboo rod, split at the end from frequent use like the pitchfork of the devil himself. He knew he had to run and hide, but his feet felt nailed to the ground as his mother's shining eyes drew closer and closer, till they swallowed up the entire world. Just then he would wake up, and once he had come to his senses a little, he would climb out of bed in his sweat-soaked pajamas and sneak into the kitchen for a smoke, walking on tiptoes to keep from waking his wife.

The only guarantee of eternal youth is an early death. Mrs. Ilona Vendyšová, née Horváthová, passed away at age thirty-six. Her fifteen-year-old son grieved for her immensely. He had always hoped his mother would live to a ripe old age, so he could walk her around the park in the sunshine on Sundays and holidays. Even if she was wheelchair-bound, twisted with arthritis, and entirely dependent on his help—he would offer it gladly, with all his heart.

But she never gave him the pleasure. On the contrary her magical power, unexhausted by long life and undiminished by age, lingered on in the realm of those mysterious forces that incomprehensibly yet undoubtedly intrude upon the fate of the living. Long after her death, Mrs. Horváthová still influenced the life of her son, his relationships with women, and even his working methods.

The handsome Lieutenant Vendyš developed a

complex system of defenses and inhibitions in rela-
tion to women, most clearly embodied in his choice of
life partner. The younger Mrs. Vendyšová was a timid
mouse, bland in appearance and personality, who
adored her husband slavishly and never got over her
amazement at the fact that he had chosen her. It was a
happy marriage.

The working methods he employed, on the other
hand, were relatively simple. He was extremely well
aware—based on his experience on the receiving end,
so to speak—of the impact of his eyes. They were an
invaluable aid for a cop, and using them as his foun-
dation he had worked out a procedure that, although
primitive, proved effective in the vast majority of
cases. Unlike his fellow investigators, he didn't shine
a light into the faces of people he questioned. Instead,
he always made sure his own face was well lit, stared
intently into the eyes of the suspect, and tapped his
pencil against the table in rhythm to each precisely and
pointedly worded question he asked. Sooner or later
the suspect got nervous and began to panic. Vendyš
could tell exactly when the tension reached its peak
and change tactics on a dime: he would drop his eyes to
the desk—or, depending, put on sunglasses—set aside
his pencil, smile and switch to a calm, friendly tone
of voice. The relief suspects typically felt in response

amounted to a state of mild shock. Like the dimwitted gratitude of a cow sent to slaughter, then by some miracle spared the axe. At which point most men spilled their guts about everything they could remember, and often out of sheer diligence they would even make something up. It was the only disadvantage of this approach, albeit comparatively slight.

Vendyš investigated cases of murder, assault, and grievous bodily harm. He didn't have any political assignments, so he could afford the luxury of taking his job seriously. He just wanted to ascertain the facts, or, as he somewhat reluctantly put it to himself, he wanted the truth to come out. The plain truth, so anyone could understand: who, when, how. And sometimes also why. The last one wasn't strictly necessary, but it was the one he found most interesting: the endless variety of reasons why people killed other people in a country where murder rarely brought any financial gain.

The murder of Captain Nedoma, however, was a special case, and Lieutenant Vendyš knew there was another investigation proceeding in parallel with his on a higher level, since Nedoma's assignments may not have been that important, but they were still considered classified. *Thank God that's none of my business*, Vendyš thought. *I stick to my own affairs.*

He had been as diligent as ever in preparing for the

investigation. It certainly wasn't his fault that his time-tested method had failed during the first questioning on Saturday afternoon. The Horizon manager wasn't one to be easily shaken. She appeared calm and nonchalant sitting in the lieutenant's unwelcoming office, her seven-mile legs in lizard-skin pumps (*Where did she smuggle those in from*, Vendyš wondered; *she sure as heck didn't get them here*) elegantly crossed, smiling widely as her gray-green eyes stared straight into his. An image of a beautiful mulatto flashed through the lieutenant's mind . . . from some island or something, where had he seen that?

He rapped the desk with his pencil once, then let it drop. It rolled off the desk onto the floor. He was about to bend down and grab it, but then, realizing it would diminish his authority in the eyes of the witness to see him fumbling around on the floor, he decided to just let it roll off into the corner and drummed his fingers on the tabletop instead. The manager maintained her easygoing smile, though with a touch of a smirk to it. Vendyš glanced at his nails and folded his hands in his lap. *Who does this broad think she is?* he thought. *I'll bet that dress comes from Paris, too—no way she got it here. But I'll teach her a lesson. Next time she flies somewhere, I'll make sure there's a strip search waiting for her when she gets back!* Thinking about it just rattled him more. He blushed a little, realizing he was on a slippery slope. The situation called for radical action. He had no choice but to abandon his usual routine. You have to adapt when it comes to exceptional circumstances. He sighed to himself and opened the folder on his desk. Maybe the strictly official approach would be more effective.

"Comrade Manager, our preliminary investigation suggests that your cinema is in quite a shambles."

Lieutenant Vendyš shot her a glance from under his brow, but she just sat snugly perched on her chair, smiling at him as his palms broke out in sweat. He screwed up his face in concentration and forged ahead: "Let's take it from the top. According to the testimony of eyewitnesses, during the critical period, between seven thirty and eight thirty P.M., Comrade Vránová left the Horizon and returned about half an hour later. Libuše Pařízková went out in front of the building to meet her fiancé, Petr Krátký, and was gone for about twenty minutes. Helena Nováková went out to buy aspirin from an after-hours pharmacy about five minutes' walk away, but was gone nearly half an hour. As for you, Comrade Manager, your husband came to pick you up in his vehicle about fifteen minutes after the start of the show"—pregnant pause followed by an ineffective glint of black—"and you didn't return to work after that." The lieutenant shut the folder.

"Yes," the manager said sweetly, "that's correct."

Vendyš waited to see if she would add anything further, but she left it at that. He fumbled around on the desk a while, out of habit, then remembered that his pencil was on the floor in the corner.

"Wouldn't you agree, Comrade Manager," he said in a tone verging on rude, "that employees should remain in the workplace during working hours?"

The manager pulled a mirror out of her lizard-skin bag, ran a hand through her hair, pursed her lips, and examined herself with that unnatural look women tend to assume when they're in front of a mirror; that casual expression that makes it clear they're anxious to see what they look like, but at the same time they want to make sure they look as good as possible.

"As I understand it," the manager said serenely, tucking the mirror back in her bag, "you're investigating a murder, not the work ethic in our cinema. I know nothing about the murder and I'm responsible to the head office for conditions at our workplace. I've received no complaint from them. But for your information, our staff are entitled to breaks and typically choose to take them during the period you call critical. Where and how they spend them is their business, not mine. So assuming that's all you want to know, I should be getting back to work. Your people have caused a considerable stir and I'm needed there, if you don't mind . . ."

"Just a moment," Vendyš said. "Captain Nedoma investigated the murder of that boy in your cinema. All your employees met with him. Would you happen to know if any of them were in contact with him afterwards?"

"The private affairs of my personnel are no concern of mine. I don't have the slightest idea."

She rose from her seat.

"May I go now?" she asked impatiently.

"All right," Vendyš conceded. "I'll come by Monday afternoon around three to have a word with your staff. Please see to it that we have a room where we won't be disturbed."

"You can use my office. I'll make arrangements."

The lieutenant stood up and walked the manager to the door, then stood a while watching as she strutted down the hideous gray hall on her high heels.

Some people were like those flowers that grow inside bottles, he thought. They made their own environment and carried it with them, wherever they went. Nothing got through to them.

He shut the door and returned to his desk. The

telephone rang. He picked it up and growled his name. A young voice on the other end said, "We've got the autopsy results. You'll get a written report through official channels, of course, but there's something I thought might interest you, so I figured I'd give you a ring. Besides his dinner and some beer, the man had a touch of barbiturate in him. Not a big enough dose to kill him, or even to do any harm. Just the right amount for a nice little nap. You interested?"

"Why not," Vendyš said, and hung up the phone lost in thought.

"Comrade Lieutenant, sir, with your permission, I'm pleased to offer you the following full report in order as it happened." It was early Monday morning and Sergeant Koloušek sat in Vendyš's office, sweating eagerly. The chair beneath him was only wide enough to support a portion of his prodigious rear end. His light brown eyes were sunk into his pudgy cheeks like raisins in a cake, and his tiny upturned nose was the kind people used to refer to as "pert" on little girls. He had three fleshy chins, and dimpled, roly-poly arms with skin as smooth as an infant's. He wore an expression of simpleminded kindness, with an overlay of helplessness that led many people to feel an instinctive sympathy toward him and go out of their way to indulge him. Dealing with him was like dealing with a huge baby who couldn't cope in this cruel world without the help of kind people. Sergeant Koloušek produced superb results at work and was the envy of all his shrewder and better-looking colleagues.

The sight of Koloušek as he gave his report—moist lips puckered with effort, running his thick index finger over the lines in his notebook—drove Vendyš insane. Every time he looked at him, he imagined Koloušek squeezed into a flask of alcohol sealed with an enormous stopper, oblivious to his situation, forehead fervently creased, thin strands of hair undulating in the fluid, gesturing to his beat-up notepad . . .

This time, too, Koloušek had barely begun his report when Vendyš got up from his desk and went to stand at the window, with his back facing the room. Even with the utmost effort, he could either listen to Koloušek or look at him. Both at once was more than he could take.

"Right, so Marie Vránová ate dinner Friday evenin' at the Little Bears. They all know her there, 'specially the comrade waitress that served her that night, and also the comrade waiter—he actually told me he'd been involved with her, so to speak, a while back, if you get what I mean. Anyways, so Vránová comes rushin' in, sayin' she's starvin' and in a hurry, and orders the beef in cream sauce. S'posedly she doesn't go there that often. Doesn't surprise me," Koloušek added uncharacteristically. "Usher like her, after all, how much can she make, right, Comrade Lieutenant, to be goin' out eatin' dinners on the town? Gal like her, ordinarily, only goes to the pub when a guy's payin' her way, if you get what I mean."

Vendyš detected an aggrieved tone in Koloušek's voice, a hint of envy.

"But anyways they said she just picked at her food and left half on the plate. Which strikes me as suspicious, seein' how hungry she said she was."

Koloušek looked up at the lieutenant's back and waited a moment, but getting no response, he continued. "Accordin' to a statement from Božena Šulcová at the Black Cat snack bar, Vránová exited the Horizon and turned right on Steep Street 'bout five minutes past eight and a few minutes after quarter past she was already at the pub, so she must've walked by the car with Nedoma inside—the comrade captain, that is—but she couldn't've stuck around long. Course how much time do you need to stick a knife in a man's ribs, right?"

He looked up at Vendyš again. *Boy, that Vendyš is one strange bug*, he thought. *Here I am doing my best, giving the guy an airtight report, and he just stands there like a statue. Talking to somebody's back, what kinda teamwork is that?* Koloušek sighed to himself and bent his head over his notes. His chunky index finger set out again on its zigzag journey down the page.

"She re-entered the Horizon from the other side, via Perštýn. Got that confirmed from Petr Krátký, who happened to be on his way to a date with Libuše Pařízková when he ran into Vránová on the corner and walked her back to work. Comrade Šulcová saw 'em too. I tell you, that broad don't miss a thing. She's got eyes everywhere," Sergeant Koloušek said admiringly. He paused again and cast an accusing glance at Vendyš's back.

"So 'bout five minutes later, Pařízková comes runnin' out. She strolls down the street with Krátký a while, then they cross over and head to the Praha cafeteria. They say that's their spot for potato pancakes, seein' as Šulcová doesn't serve 'em, but if you ask me the real reason is they know Šulcová's got her antenna up and they like to stay outta range. Anyways, Pařízková gets back to the cinema 'bout twenty minutes later. But in the meantime Nováková steps out to the pharmacy on the corner, buys a tube of aspirin, and then for the next fifteen minutes or so, I'm in the dark."

Vendyš finally turned around. "What do you mean, in the dark?"

Koloušek squirmed. He lowered his eyes and ran a hand through the peach fuzz on his scalp. "What she says, Comrade Lieutenant, is she went out for a walk to clear her head. They gave her a glass of water at the drugstore so she could take the aspirin right away. But nobody saw her after that. I mean, I wasn't able to verify that anybody saw her. Course fifteen minutes, that'd do the trick. Two left turns from the pharmacy, catch up with the comrade captain, take care of business, and go right back the same way. Šulcová wouldn't've spotted her, 'less she went back in the cinema. The vehicle was out of Šulcová's range, so she's got nothin' for us."

"Of course that assumes Nováková knew that Comrade Captain Nedoma was there. And that she had a motive. In any case, it could have been her. Nobody else left the cinema?" Vendyš asked.

"Well, Šulcová says Kouřimská stopped in a little before eight and bought some smokes, but she says she didn't go out. Then there's that fella Šípek. Šulcová says she noticed him mopin' around outside, and he admits he was waitin' for Nováková. That was around ten, though. He's keen on Nováková, but Šulcová says—"

"Hell's bells, is that the only information we've got? Just what Šulcová says?"

Koloušek wriggled in his seat again.

"Oh, I got lots of information, Comrade Lieutenant. But Šulcová's reliable. She's the kinda witness I wish I had more of. I'd stake my life on what she says. 'Course I can't rule out that Šípek went by earlier, left, and came back. But there's no proof for it so far, at least if what Šulcová—"

"Dammit!" Vendyš shouted, but then regained his composure. "Forgive me, Comrade. Please, go on," he said, turning back to the window.

Koloušek sniffed and pouted. "Look, Comrade Lieutenant, I undertook an extensive investigation and I got a slew of credible eyewitness testimony. Thanks to the cashier, for instance, I tracked down the addresses of several audience members from that evening. Most of 'em regular customers that live in the area. Pensioners and so forth who got nothing better to do than go to the movies. Sometimes they go see the same one three times."

Koloušek got the impression the back was growing impatient and quickly went on. "I spoke to some of 'em. An old couple, the Soukups, Vilém and Amálie, were practically the first ones to enter the theater. Right when they opened the doors, at seven thirty.

They had cheap seats in the second row and they said nobody went out the emergency exits on either side of the screen. There's bright lights over the door on the outside, so if anyone opened 'em during the show, it would've lit up the whole house. But they both swear nobody went out that way, even before the show. I also questioned six other individuals, and they all said the same thing: emergency exits were shut the whole time."

This time Kloušek's pause was so suggestive, the lieutenant had to respond.

"That's critical information," he said. "Good work, Comrade."

Kloušek beamed. His complexion, the color of a baby's bottom with a mild rash, turned even pinker. Finally he'd received the recognition he was looking for.

"I got one other important item to report: Comrade Nedomová." He announced it as if he were unveiling a monument. "Comrade Nedomová went to dinner that night at the Wallenstein Palace with one Bořivoj Šíma, an accountant at Drutěva, the manufacturing cooperative. They arrived at seven and left just before eight. According to Šíma, they went for a stroll around Malá Strana afterwards, and sometime around ten he drove her home in his Fiat, which was parked on Malá Strana Square. In other words, if push came to shove, they could easily've made it over to Steep Street—'cept, of course, nobody saw 'em. In my opinion, if you don't mind, Comrade Lieutenant, Nedomová is our number-one suspect."

Vendyš recalled how cleverly Mrs. Nedomová had directed his attention to the Horizon, and his impression of her as better suited to the role of brave, dignified widow than mistress divorcée. Who knew how much bitterness had built up inside her over the years? It was just a pity that Koloušek shared his opinion. Everything in Vendyš rebelled at the thought that he might agree with that slug on anything. He turned, strode back to his desk, and retook his seat.

"When you searched the cinema, did you find anything, any tiny thing at all, that seemed unusual?" Vendyš asked.

Koloušek flipped through his notebook. "You know, Comrade Lieutenant, you find all kindsa crap after a screening: handkerchiefs, combs, unmatched gloves . . ."

"Anything *unusual*," Vendyš said through clenched teeth.

"Well, prob'ly the only thing was some scissors stuck behind the mirror in the ladies' room. No prints on 'em, nobody knew where they came from, and there's no way to know how long they were in there, could've been even a month. Cleaning lady didn't know any-thing. You know the type, old granny . . ."

"That'll do," Vendyš said.

Koloušek shut his notebook, wrapped a rubber band around it, and sat up straight so he could tuck it into his pants pocket. "That's all I have for now, Comrade Lieutenant," he said.

With a supreme effort, Vendyš forced himself to look into the light brown raisins. "Thank you, Com-rade. Continue with your investigation."

Monday at 3:15 P.M., the manager of the Horizon walked out of her office holding a glossy French fash-ion magazine. "Marie? Go ahead, you're first," she said, and went to sit in the smoking lounge.

Marie knocked politely and opened the door. Lieu-tenant Vendyš, wearing a hardened expression, sat behind the desk crowded with elegant trinkets. A man with short-cropped blond hair and a look of listless-ness on his alcoholic face sat hunched over a notepad in a low armchair by the coffee table in the corner. Marie took two steps in and stopped. She didn't have on her shapeless usher's uniform today, the black broadcloth smock with HORIZON CINEMA stitched in red thread on the pocket. Instead she was garbed in a clingy knit dress with a plunging neckline and her sheerest nylons. Her bangs were combed down over her forehead and her lashes were so black and curly, her circular, dark brown eyes looked like little round centipedes.

Marie walked up to the desk and smiled. The centipedes wriggled their legs.

"Have a seat, Comrade," Vendyš said, motioning to the chair on the other side of the desk.

Marie lowered herself into it, gyrating to maximum effect, crossed her legs, and put on a face that showed she was eager to please.

"Ahem," Vendyš said, tapping his pencil on the desk. "Comrade Vránová, could you tell us about your relationship with Captain Nedoma? I warn you, we have our own information, so there's no point trying to deny anything."

"But, Captain, sir . . ."

"Comrade Lieutenant. Lieutenant Vendyš."

"Why, I wouldn't dream of it. Anyway, what's there to deny? Me and Václav, the comrade captain, that is, we had a, well, what do you call it . . . we were goin' steady, you know? But I haven't even laid eyes on him now in over two months, cross my heart, Comrade Captain . . ."

"Lieutenant," growled Vendyš.

". . . and if anybody told you different, they were lying. I'll swear to you right here on the spot, if you want."

"Can you tell me why you broke up?" Vendyš said hastily.

"Oh, you know how it is. His wife found out and you know I'm not the type to break up a marriage, 'specially when there's kids involved. So we each went our own way, no hard feelings. Happens every day, right? Wouldn't you say, Comrade Captain?"

"Lieutenant. Describe for me then what you did last Friday night. Between seven and nine, say."

Wriggling her centipedes, Marie rested her chin in her palm and her elbow on her knee, edging up her skirt in the process. She thought a moment. "I guess till about eight, maybe a few minutes after, I was here at the Horizon, showin' people to their seats. Then when the show started, I decided to go to the Little Bears for some dinner."

"Do you go there often?" Vendyš asked.

"Why, surely you jest, Comrade Captain." Marie smiled. "Only if someone invites me . . ." She fixed Vendyš with her centipedes and paused meaningfully. Vendyš fumed, banging his pencil down against the desktop. Marie, startled, went on: "Ordinarily I bring something from home, some bread and salami, what have you. Either that or I pop upstairs to the snack bar. Líba brews coffee for us here at the concession stand. But on Friday morning I was tidying up my flat and all of a sudden I looked and saw it was time for me to skedaddle to work, so I didn't even eat lunch. Then by nighttime I was so hungry I thought I was gonna faint, so I figured I'd just break the bank and treat myself to a proper din-din. For a change."

"How do you have your evening breaks set up among the employees? I assume you don't all go out at once?"

"Of course not, Comrade Cap—"

"Lieutenant."

"Well, like I said before, most of the time we don't even go out, but when we do, we have to take turns, right? I mean, we can't all disappear at once. And I knew Líba—that is, Comrade Pařízková—had a date with Petr Krátký—that is, her fiancé—so I wanted to get back as fast as I could. So I ran off to the pub, had my dinner, and came straight back. And on the way I ran into Petr, who was on his way to meet Líba, and he walked me back here," Marie said. She turned to the blond party boy at the coffee table. "Did you get all that down, sir? I mean, Comrade . . . ?"

"Dolejš. Comrade Dolejš," Vendyš said mechanically.

Marie folded her hands in her lap, took a deep breath and, gathering up her courage, looked squarely into Vendyš's coal-black eyes. The main thing now was utter calm. *Here it comes.*

"Comrade Vránová," Vendyš said, his eyes piercing the center of her brown beetles like pins. He drummed his pencil on the desktop like a march for a condemned man making his way to the gallows. "Comrade Nedoma's car was already parked on Steep Street when you passed through. You must have noticed it."

"Matter of fact, I didn't. Look, Captain, sir—I mean, Comrade Lieutenant," she quickly corrected herself, reacting to the flash of annoyance in Vendyš's eyes. "How many cars do you think *you'd* notice running down a street at night, especially one with lighting as lousy as that one? I mean, how many complaints've there been about it already? Just last month there was a pensioner with a wooden leg who—"

"Hold up, Comrade Vránová, now wait a minute. Don't tell me you don't recognize the comrade captain's car."

"I recognize it all right, but it's not like I'm an expert on cars. There must be a million old clunkers crawlin' around Prague. Maybe if it was some big schmancy mobile I might've noticed. Besides, Václav—I mean, Captain Nedoma—only took me for a ride in it two or three times. We didn't go too far, usually, just from here to my flat and—"

"Comrade Vránová," Vendyš said firmly. "We'll find out the truth eventually, no matter what, so you might as well tell us now and save yourself the trouble."

Marie tilted her head to the side and gave him a fetching look while dropping a shoulder to show off her cleavage to best advantage.

Vendyš suppressed a satisfied smile. That's how he liked it. His method was working, as usual. The girl had tried every floozy trick in the book and finally it was dawning on her it wasn't going to work. She was scared out of her wits and losing her nerve. She didn't know which way to turn. She was ripe to come clean.

"Listen," the lieutenant said warmly, switching tack. "I'm on your side. If you start lying now, you'll only make things worse for yourself. We appreciate it when people confess. It could really help you, and I myself—"

"But, Comrade Captain," Marie exclaimed, jumping out of her chair. "Don't tell me you suspect *me* of killing him? Why would I wanna do that? There was nothing messy about our breakup. We parted ways and said good-bye like decent people. If you know everything, I'm sure you also know I haven't laid eyes on him in over two months. Look," Marie said, suddenly changing tone. She sat back down, leaned forward, and rested her chin on the edge of the desk, so her permed and perfumed head was right under Vendyš's nose. "Look, Comrade Lieutenant," she said solemnly. "If I had to stab every guy I ever slept with . . ."

"All right, fine, fine!" Vendyš said, rocking back in his chair away from her.

Marie fixed him with a meaningful look to signal her statement was over as far as she was concerned, then leaned back from the desk, sat up straight, pulled her skirt down over her knees, and put on a prim face that said, *I hope we understand each other now.*

There was a minute or two of silence. Vendyš stared absently at the green leather writing pad in front of him. Then he reached into his pocket and took out a small pair of pointy scissors.

"Do you know who these belong to? Have you ever seen them before?"

Marie looked surprised. She took them from the lieutenant's hand and examined them.

"I must've seen at least a thousand pairs of scissors like this. I got some just like these at home. For my nails and stuff. But I don't have a clue who these belong to. Cross my heart." She turned to the stenographer. "I swear I don't know a thing about those scissors or who they belong to," she stated slowly and emphatically. "Did you get that down?"

She laid the scissors on the desk. "What've they got

to do with it anyway?" she asked. "I thought he got stuck with a knife?"

Lieutenant Vendyš tapped his pencil on the desk again. "Thank you, Comrade Vránová. That will be all for now. You can go."

Marie stood and made her way out with a slow, undulating step. The stenographer raised his rheumy red eyes from his notepad, following her with a vacant look till she exited the office, then just stared at the door.

"Dolejš," Lieutenant Vendyš said in disgust. "Call Nováková in here for me."

Vendyš studied Nedoma's files and notes over the weekend. He knew Nedoma had been trying tirelessly, without any luck, to prove Helena Nováková was engaged in some as yet unidentified type of espionage, or at the very least that she'd had contact with individuals who were involved in such activities. Nedoma's reports, at any rate the ones he had access to, were superficial and incomplete—evidence more of the captain's sloppiness and narrow thinking than of any criminal acts or complicity on Nováková's part. Vendyš also attempted to obtain some new information about the cause of Karel Novák's suicide, but none of the officials he approached could offer any insight into the mystery.

In any event, Nováková may have had serious reason to get rid of Nedoma, and Vendyš, who was neither stupid nor sloppy, systematically set to work. If Novák's wife had anything on her conscience, he would uncover it.

Based on his investigation so far, the lieutenant, as was his custom, had developed a fairly well-defined notion of the woman who had attracted so much attention from State Security, so when she walked into the room, he was stunned.

Garbed in her black work smock, Helena appeared almost shockingly thin and pale; her face, with deep circles of insomnia under her eyes, looked tiny and helpless as a child's. As she stepped up to the desk, Vendyš observed the gently chiseled lines at the corners of her mouth and around her eyes, like some secret code. He'd never seen so much silent pain and resignation in a person's face.

"Hello," he said politely. "Please, have a seat." Helena sat down in the chair on the other side of the desk. Dolejš staggered back to the corner, flopped into the armchair, took out his pad and pencil, and stretched out his legs.

Helena sat motionless. *Like a statue*, Lieutenant Vendyš thought. *Carved of alabaster. She could probably sit like that forever.*

The lieutenant intentionally took his time. He leaned back, fixing his eyes on the white face with the downcast eyes. Minutes slipped by. The note-taker began to doze off, sliding even further down in his chair. Helena didn't stir. Vendyš rapped the desk with his pencil and Dolejš woke with a snort, but Helena didn't even lift her head. Vendyš sighed to himself. "Comrade Nováková, you knew Comrade Captain Nedoma, did you not?"

"I saw him here at the cinema," Helena said. "He was investigating the murder of Josef Vrba."

"Did you ever meet him again after that?"

"No. Never."

"Or even see him?"

Helena hesitated.

Lieutenant Vendyš said mildly, "I've just had a talk with Comrade Vránová. She told us about her relation-ship with Captain Nedoma. So please, speak as freely as you wish."

Helena replied as calmly as she had the first time. "I saw him just two or three times on the street here, in front of the cinema. Waiting for her, I guess. Apart from that, I never met him."

"Where were you Friday night between seven thirty and eight thirty?"

"Here at the Horizon. Then at about ten after

eight—I'm not sure exactly—I went out. I had a head-
ache all afternoon. I went to buy some aspirin at the
pharmacy on the corner."

"Were all the other ushers here when you left?"

Helena thought a moment. "I'm not positive, but I
think Marie Vránová left a while before me."

"And you came straight back here from the pharmacy?"

"No. I walked down the street for about fifteen minutes. I already told all this to the officer who—"

"I realize that," Vendyš said. "I just needed to con-
firm it. This is just a preliminary investigation. We're
going to have to ask you about everything a few more
times. There's always a chance you might remember
something that can help us. When you were walking
down the street, did you meet anybody you know?"

"No, not that I recall."

"What were you wearing?"

Helena squinted in concentration. "I think . . . the
same thing as today. Yes, a blue-and-white striped skirt
and a dark blue woolen sweater."

"Maybe we can find someone who noticed you to con-
firm your statement. If anything at all comes to mind   we
have to verify everything, I'm sure you understand. Please
just let me know. Your boss has my phone number."

Vendyš studied her again for a moment. Then said

impulsively, "Tell me, Comrade Nováková. What do you think about the murder?"

The expression on Helena's face didn't change. She probably didn't realize what an unorthodox question it was. It took her some time to respond. The note-taker, who apparently had taught himself not to waste a single moment on the job, had nodded off again.

"Such a brutal murder," Helena said at last, "could only have been done by someone genuinely insane, truly deranged. Someone who hated or feared him so much that nothing mattered to them anymore. Not their own life or anyone else's. Captain Nedoma must have hurt somebody badly. Either that or he was about to."

Lieutenant Vendyš sat staring at her, thinking. He had a funny feeling the answer was close at hand. All it would take was two or three questions. But for the life of him, he couldn't figure out what they were.

He reached into his pocket and held out his hand. "I don't suppose you know who these scissors belong to?"

For the first time Helena turned to face him. She took a cursory glance at the scissors. "They could be mine."

Vendyš leaned forward. "Could you say for sure?"

"I carry some just like them in my handbag. If they aren't there, I must have lost them. In which case they could be mine."

"Where is your handbag now? In the cloakroom?"
Helena nodded.

"Dolejš," said the lieutenant. "Go ask Comrade
Vránová if she could bring in that handbag."

Dolejš shuffled to the door and pushed it open into
the hallway. A few minutes later he returned with a
dark blue handbag, which he placed on the desk in
front of Helena, then headed back to his chair. He
collapsed into it exhausted, but with a sense of satis-
faction. *It's hard work being a spook,* he thought. *Major
responsibility.*

Helena dug through her bag and pulled out a pair of
scissors identical to the ones Vendyš held in his hand.
She set them down on the desk.

"There, you see," she said. "They're exactly the
same."

"All right. You can put them away," Vendyš said dis-
appointedly. "And you can go now. Thank you."

As the door closed behind Helena, Vendyš leaned
back and yawned widely. Some case this was. Damn
thing wasn't going anywhere.

"Who've we got next, Dolejš?" he asked grouchily.

4

⁓

ALL DAY THE sky kept dropping lower and lower, until evening when the first autumn rain let loose. Vendyš trudged to the top of Steep Street, hands dug into his raincoat pockets, and stopped with his back to the glass wall of the snack bar, where Božena stood rocking behind the counter. He looked out at the short, dimly lit lane where they had found the old blue Škoda on Friday, and thought hard. Rain streamed down the inside of his collar, but he paid it no attention.

After two weeks of investigation and questioning he hardly knew any more than he had when he first saw the victim. The murder weapon hadn't provided a single clue. An ordinary kitchen knife, used for cutting meat, one of two types produced in Czechoslovakia, available at any hardware or department store as well as some supermarkets. There were hundreds of them sold every day. The knife was brand-new, so just to cover all the bases Vendyš had sent a couple of detectives around the shops to ask if anyone happened to remember one of the suspects buying a knife like that recently, but as he had anticipated, it didn't lead anywhere. Almost everywhere someone remembered "a shortish man and his wife," "a young lady who looked like she was buying it for her hope chest," "a heavyset brunette woman in a blue dress," but as soon as the detectives flashed the photos of the people connected to the case, the salespeople shook their heads. He didn't expect anything different; the killer could have bought the knife months ago and kept it hidden at home till the opportunity presented itself.

Vendyš wiped away the rain sliding down his nose. Steep Street was like an empty auditorium after a performance, with Vendyš the late-coming spectator who could only guess at what had taken place.

There were only two possibilities. Either the killer had driven here in the car with Nedoma, who by that time could barely keep his eyes open anymore, sat with him a while, maybe had a little chat while he watched him fall asleep, then plunged the knife into his chest, got out of the car, and disappeared. On average about one and a quarter people an hour walked down the little street after dark. The killer could have slipped away unobserved without too much trouble. The question was whether any passerby would have consciously noted someone casually climbing out of a parked car, even assuming they did see it.

The other possibility was that Nedoma had driven here alone, fallen asleep behind the wheel, and the killer, who somehow knew he would be there, slipped into the car, killed the captain, and sauntered off. It could've been anyone. In his line of work, Nedoma must have had plenty of enemies, and Vendyš had managed to track down and investigate a number of people who had it in for Nedoma, but the result was zero-point-zero. He couldn't assume the killer just coincidentally stumbled across the car, saw Nedoma asleep, pulled out the huge knife he just happened to have in his pocket—no, coincidence played no role in this. Whoever killed Nedoma had mixed a barbiturate into his drink beforehand. Somebody who knew him well, who'd sat somewhere and talked with him. Definitely not some bad guy Nedoma had put the screws on once upon a time. An image of the tall gray-haired man in the beige suit Vendyš had seen standing on the corner across the street just after the murder was discovered flitted across the screen of the lieutenant's consciousness.

Moving along. Obviously no fingerprints. A killer would have to be pretty stupid to work without gloves nowadays. Everyone knew the drill from all those movies and murder mysteries. It was pretty convenient for the ladies this year especially, all walking around in those crocheted gloves. A fashion tailor-made for murderers. The only prints inside the car, besides Nedoma's, belonged to his younger daughter, who he'd driven to the health center with tonsillitis just the day before. Nothing on the knife of course, and just one big smudge on the door handle, from the perpetrator running his gloved fingers over it.

Another mystery was what Nedoma had been doing on Steep Street and what time he had arrived. No matter how hard he tried, Vendyš still hadn't been able to pin down where Nedoma was earlier that evening. About half past five he'd left the office and driven over to Štajdls' in Malá Strana for a beer and a frankfurter. At six fifteen he paid and left. Didn't talk to anyone and no one sat at his table. It was still early, the restaurant was half empty, and the captain was a familiar face. From then till nine o'clock, when Officer

Zemánek spotted the car as he was walking his beat, no one had a clue where Nedoma had been. Zemánek was also the one who noticed, on his second pass at quarter to ten, that the car was still parked in the same spot and the driver was still behind the wheel. He figured it must be some guy sleeping off a hangover, peeked in the window, and saw the knife handle with a long dark line running down the driver's white shirt.

At first it had seemed logical that the location of the killing must have some connection to Nedoma's complicated relationships with the Horizon staff. But in spite of his strenuous investigation and inquiries, Vendyš hadn't been able to turn up any concrete link, let alone a sufficient motive. Vránová had peacefully parted ways with Nedoma a while back, and there was no indication of any stormy aftermath to their affair. Even Mrs. Nedomová, who was obviously well aware of her spouse's infidelities, said his relationship with Vránová had long been "case closed."

Kouřimská, as Vendyš had discovered from Nedoma's files and confirmed through personal questioning, was a low-level paid informant. Nedoma himself had planted her in the cinema, and he was a welcome source of income for her, so his death had caused her a considerable loss—she gained nothing from it. The lieutenant had scrutinized her activity in detail. It

couldn't be ruled out that some seemingly trivial piece
of information that she supplied to Nedoma had led
to his murder. Vendyš was convinced, however, that
while the bits of news and gossip Kouřimská supplied the captain with may have occasionally come in
handy, they never amounted to anything substantial.
Her main assignment was to keep an eye on Helena
Nováková, who, in view of the unfortunate case of
Karel Novák, was of course highly suspect. It also
turned out that Nováková, via Kouřimská, at Nedoma's instructions, had been introduced to Comrade
Hrůza himself and seen him for a period of time.
Vendyš zeroed in on the trail like a hawk. But all his
efforts led only to negative conclusions. Nováková
had no idea Nedoma was spying on her, and ultimately, Vendyš concluded, she had nothing to hide.
It wasn't surprising that Nedoma had suspected her,
but clearly it was a false lead. Helena Nováková was
the embodiment of innocence.

Kouřimská had also notified Nedoma about Šípek,
and Nedoma had seen to it that Security gave him a
thorough grilling more than once. This yielded a thick
and utterly worthless file proving nothing except
that Šípek was in love with Nováková and followed
her along like a puppy dog. Šípek wasn't surprised to
learn Nováková was being watched, though it never

crossed his mind that Nedoma—whom for that matter he'd never met—or Kouřimská had anything to do with it.

Eventually Vendyš realized the trail he had been nudged onto so cleverly by Mrs. Nedomová, though it appeared promising, led to a dead end. Too bad he couldn't disprove her alibi. Not yet anyway.

Vendyš's shoes were beginning to leak. He shifted his weight back and forth, glancing across the street again. The tall slim man in the beige suit. What had he been doing here that day?

Yes, at first glance all the evidence pointed to the Horizon. But what if it was only an optical illusion? What if the murderer had deliberately set it up to divert attention away from himself? Vendyš had the cinema and its staff under constant surveillance, and his henchmen hadn't failed to notice that Comrade Hrůza turned up in the vicinity of the Horizon late at night with surprising frequency. Always alone; never met with or said a word to anyone. Vendyš wasn't informed about what "the other guys" were up to, but he knew Nedoma made himself available to cooperate with Hrůza, occasionally taking on confidential and probably pretty unsavory assignments.

Vendyš let out a sigh. The ground was giving way beneath his feet. He knew which way the line pointed and knew he couldn't follow it. A cold trickle of rain ran down the inside of his collar, and it suddenly hit him what a dark and gloomy day it was and how empty and meaningless human life was. He turned and walked into the snack bar.

Božena's face lit up. She toddled rapidly to the end of the counter where Vendyš stood, leaning his elbows on the counter.

"Good day," the lieutenant said with exaggerated courtesy. "One small vodka, please." He only drank on special occasions, but today he needed it, body and soul.

Božena filled a glass to the rim and waited expectantly, focusing the full force of her intelligence on him. Maybe the handsome lieutenant would ask her another question. She felt a delicious shudder of anticipation, an immense desire to call attention to herself, ingratiate herself, show off her quick wit and feminine intuition. Sharp-lookin' fella like him might think, *Well, she's no beauty queen, but she's definitely something special. Not too many women out there with powers of observation like hers. I ought to pay more attention to her. I'm sure she'd be a big help in my work.*

"Comrade Šulcová," Vendyš said, sipping his vodka cautiously to make sure he didn't choke. "I'd like to ask you one more time. On Friday, just before eight o'clock, Mrs. Kouřimská came in here to buy a pack of cigarettes. Did you see her arrive and leave that day?"

Božena thought a moment.

"No, sir. Girls come into work at half past two and I'm not on till three. They're all downstairs by the time I get in. 'Tween the matinee and evening shows—say, 'bout six to seven thirty, then again after eight—sometimes they wander outside or come in here for a bite or whatever. I didn't notice Kouřimská till she was right at the counter. You know how it gets, Comrade Lieutenant. By that time my head's in a whirl. She was a little outta breath from runnin' up the stairs, so she just grabbed her smokes and ran back down. Didn't go out, I know that for sure. I would've noticed."

Božena pulled a box from under the counter, poured a heap of cookies onto a thick porcelain plate, and slid it in front of Vendyš.

"Thank you," said the lieutenant. He took one, bit off a mouthful, and munched absently. Božena didn't take her eyes off of him.

"You probably don't remember, but there's one more tiny detail I'd like to ask about. Well, can't hurt to try: A little later after that, when Comrade Nováková went to the pharmacy, did she happen to have a handbag with her? Do you think you remember?"

Božena closed her eyes and wrinkled her forehead.

The circuits kicked into gear and her whole face lit up. "I sure do!" she exclaimed. "I remember, all right! See, Helena's got this teeny little red bag, more like a big wallet, really. All it holds is a comb, mirror, and keys. Don't ask me where she got it, but I've always liked that thing. So I notice when I see it. And right now, if I shut my eyes"—Božena closed her eyes—"I can see Helena walkin' out that door with that little red bag in her right hand. That's all she had with her, that's it."

"Wow, that's terrific," Vendyš said. "Just terrific."

Božena shut her eyes again. In bliss.

And that meant, Vendyš mused, that Nováková definitely couldn't have had a knife as long as that on her. She wouldn't have had anyplace to hide it.

"Now if you don't mind, there's something else I'd like to ask." Vendyš took a second cookie and chewed it in silence a while, as if wondering how to put it. "Did you by any chance notice, Comrade, whether a tall slim man, middle-aged, in a light suit, passed by here that evening?"

"Grayish hair, suntanned? You bet. That's that fella that was keen on Helena, used to wait on her here, out in front. Then I guess they had it out, 'cos I haven't seen him around much lately. Was he here that Friday night? Now wait a sec . . ." Božena paused, then said slowly, "I got a feelin', yeah, he was. Never

came in the snack bar, I just used to see him walkin'
around outside . . . And he was definitely here that
night. I remember now. Saw him twice. First around
seven thirty, somewhere in there when Kouřimská
stopped by. Just caught a glimpse of him, it was
packed in here—then again later. No customers left by
then, and I look out and see all these cops pullin' up—I
mean, comrade officers—and he's standin' there on the
corner watchin', too. Maybe he was just comin' back
from the theater or something."

"Hm," Lieutenant Vendyš said, finishing his vodka.
"Maybe." He pulled out a handkerchief and ran it over
his hair, still damp from the rain. "Well, thank you
very much, Comrade Šulcová. You really have been a
terrific help to us. There aren't many people as obser-
vant as you."

He reached his hand across the counter. Božena
inserted her chubby little hand into his hard masculine
palm. Her mind went black and sparks shot through her
body. She closed her eyes and imagined herself wrapped
in a passionate embrace. A moment of utter and perfect
happiness. She couldn't have asked for more.

Božena kept her dreams small and modest. That way
they came true surprisingly often.

Vendyš walked out the glass door into the cinema
lobby, unconsciously wiping his right hand on the

inside of his pocket. A disagreeable greasy feeling remained. But his mind was on other things.

He knew he'd reached an impasse. There was just one thing left to do: take it "upstairs."

"So you don't have any proof," said the thin, inconspicuous elderly man. He sat straight as a coffin nail, rigid behind his enormous desk. Gray hair, gray skin, light blue-gray eyes. Small, sharp pupils behind rimless glasses. In fact his features were so unremarkable he blended in with his surroundings like an animal with protective coloration. *Like those moths you can't even see on the bark of a tree when you're looking right at them,* Vendyš thought. If he'd run into him on the street, he wouldn't even have noticed him.

"No, Comrade Commissioner, I don't," Vendyš said, "and I doubt I'll be able to get any until I have access to information on the full range of Comrade Nedoma's activities. In particular his collaboration with Comrade Hrůza. All I know now is it's related to several individuals employed at the Horizon. Based on what I've learned to date, it's possible Comrade Hrůza has information in his possession that could help me solve this case, particularly as concerns the motive, which still remains unclear."

The gray man behind the desk reached for his

cigarette case, slid one out, lit it, and slowly exhaled a gray cloud of smoke. Then he tightened his lips and thought a moment, silently tapping the armrest of his chair with the hand holding the cigarette.

"Repeat for me in brief, if you would, what steps you've taken so far," he said drily.

"I assume there's no need for me to go into detail on my routine investigation of Comrade Captain Nedoma's work and all of the people who might have been plotting to take his life in revenge?" He gave the old man an inquiring look and received a nod of approval. "In any case the outcome was negative. Seeing as the body was discovered next to the Horizon cinema, where the comrade captain had a variety of both official and personal interests, I concentrated my inquiry on the local staff. But as yet," Vendyš emphasized, "as yet it hasn't led to anything concrete. The comrade captain had an affair with one of the girls there that lasted several months." He coughed discreetly. "It ended on good terms some time ago. Comrade Nedomová claims the girl herself initiated the breakup. The other individual Comrade Nedoma had contact with was the informant Kouřimská. The comrade captain's death means a considerable financial loss to her. Her assignment was to keep tabs on Helena Nováková, whose husband, as you know, committed suicide in custody. Nováková's been in poor health ever since, in a state of total apathy, and I'm convinced she doesn't have any idea about the activities of either Kouřimská or Comrade Nedoma." The lieutenant paused a moment.

"That leaves Comrade Nedomová. She has a fairly strong motive: Their marriage was very bad, but the comrade captain didn't want a divorce. Problem is, we don't have a shred of evidence against her. Nobody saw her in the vicinity of the car, her fingerprints aren't there, and her alibi's solid. That's the story so far with everyone I've investigated in connection with the murder."

The gray old man behind the desk stubbed out his cigarette in a smoked-glass ashtray. Vendyš had the impression the man was fading away, dissolving into thin air, everywhere and nowhere at once.

He gave it another try.

"Comrade Commissioner," Vendyš said, now almost pleading. "There's one very fundamental piece of this whole thing I'm missing—and that is what orders Comrade Nedoma had from Comrade Hrůza. Comrade Hrůza's role in this case is too significant for me to just overlook. Of course that doesn't mean I suspect him of anything," Vendyš hastily added. "But given his presence at the scene of the crime around the time it was committed, his ongoing working and perhaps personal relationship with Comrade Nedoma, and the fact that he knew both Nováková and Kouřimská, I'm sure he'd have some relevant information for me. So with your permission, Comrade Commissioner, I'd like to request a meeting with Comrade Hrůza."

Vendyš leaned back wearily in his chair. *I did what I could*, he thought.

The gray man sat bolt upright, not blinking an eye. Then he gave Vendyš a stiff look and rattled off like a robot, "Thank you, Comrade Lieutenant. You may proceed with the investigation. Your report has been duly noted and I will advise you as soon as possible as to what steps I have taken."

One day passed into the next. Vendyš rummaged through all of his notes and statements again, calling back all the witnesses he had already questioned, as well as a whole string of new ones Koloušek desperately threw his way. He walked the streets, haunting street corners for hours, breaking into people's flats and prying into their private affairs, which inevitably turned out to have nothing to do with the case. He fought with his wife and most of his coworkers, snapping at his subordinates and insulting Koloušek ruthlessly, with no compunction at all, yet still no invitation to interview Comrade Hrůza was forthcoming.

5

DURING THE DAY the sun still showed itself occasionally, but the evenings grew rapidly longer and a cold wind kicked up at night. The summer had been unusually long, yet this year, like every year, it was still a surprise when autumn came. On her way home from work, Mrs. Kouřimská tried to recall those not-so-long-ago summer nights, when the streets were filled with people in lightweight colorful clothing, nobody felt like going home, and her walk home was a refreshing stroll she looked forward to all day long. It was hard to imagine now. It seemed like summer had floated off to some faraway island in the Pacific, and this street had never been anything other than dark and cold.

Usually she hurried to get home as soon as possible, but today for some reason she couldn't be rushed. Lately she'd felt an inexplicable fatigue creeping over her, intensifying day by day. Even sleep didn't help. She got out of bed in the morning more tired than when she got in at night. *Maybe I should stay home for a few days*, she thought. But what for? It wasn't as if she was sick, and it certainly wasn't going to help to spend more time alone. The traffic light on the corner of the embankment turned red. Mrs. Kouřimská stopped and unconsciously looked up.

Today he had on a brown coat over his light-colored suit, which made him look a little shorter, but more brawny. He stared intensely into her eyes, as always, but instead of being threatening the way it usually was, this time she detected a flash of triumphant contempt, the possessive assurance of a hunter with his finger on the trigger. The blood pounded furiously in her brain. She charged forward, before the light could change, almost straight under the wheels of a taxi. The driver poked his head out the window and shouted something at her. Mrs. Kouřimská dashed headlong across the bridge, almost to the middle, then stopped and turned around. Today, for the first time, Hrůza didn't remain on the corner, instead marching straight toward her with measured strides.

She broke into a run. *It's all over, he's going to kill me*, she thought. *Today, today is the day he's finally going to kill me*. Her stomach lurched as tiny bubbles fizzed in her head. She felt the air pressing down on her chest, and the bag slung over her shoulder suddenly weighed a ton. She let it fall to the ground, dragging it by the strap along the sidewalk. She raced ahead, bent forward, but the street was sliding out from under her feet, the ground heaving as the world turned upside down. Mrs. Kouřimská looked up at the sky and staggered dizzily. Suddenly it felt like there was an elephant resting its foot on her chest, slowly pressing down on her, with all its weight, pinning her to the ground. Something inside her head popped, like the cork flying out of a bottle of champagne, and the bubbles fizzed up and out, into the heavy autumn sky.

As the screen lit up with color and a cacophony like a flock of frightened birds filled the room, the ush ers walked out of the auditorium, carefully closing the doors behind them. The afternoon screening was under way. The manager came out of her office and

walked to the concession stand, where Líba was tally-
ing the receipts. The ushers gathered around her.

"They just called again from the hospital," the manager said, leaning against the counter. "Mrs. Kouřimská
just barely survived the first heart attack. They managed
to restore her heartbeat, the doctor said. But last night
she had another episode. The doctor asked if she has
any relatives. Do any of you know? Apparently it doesn't
look too good, so they'd like to notify the family."

Her question was met with silence. Líba pulled a
rubber band around a stack of bills, deposited them in
the register drawer, and clicked it shut.

"I don't think she's got anyone," she said. "She never
said much about herself, as we all know. But she did
mention to me once that she was all alone in the world.
Poor thing."

"Is she conscious?" Ládinka asked with red-lidded
eyes.

"Yes. And the doctor says it would do her good
to have visitors. Though they don't want crowds of
people. I'm going to go over there now and"—the
manager looked around at the half-circle of befuddled
faces—"and I'd like you to come with me, Marie. On
behalf of all the staff. We'll buy her some flowers and
bring her greetings from everyone, okay?"

The manager turned and disappeared into her

office. Marie looked at her coworkers and threw up her hands.

"Why me? I don't get it," she said, heading for the cloakroom.

"I don't either," said Ládinka. "Poor Mrs. Kouřimská. She should've been years away from a heart attack. But who knows what she's been through. And she was such a sweetheart. Never a cross word to anyone."

Helena followed Marie into the cloakroom. She already had on her coat, with a colorful knitted cap and a matching scarf tied around her collar.

"Marie," Helena said. "I'd like to come too, if I could. Mrs. Kouřimská was always kind to me. She was the one who introduced me to the man who helped Karel. Please, if you could find out whether she would see me."

"Sure thing. I think all the girls'll go and visit her, if they can. It's really weird the boss chose me. I never thought Kouřimská was all that hot on me."

Marie grabbed her gloves and bag and stepped into the hallway just as the manager closed her office door behind her.

The tram rattled up a depressing street that trickled downhill like a river of brown leaves. Marie held a bouquet of carnations in her lap, wrapped in dark green tissue paper. Every now and then she glanced uneasily at the manager, who stared straight ahead the whole way. The two women sat side by side, thinking the same thing, but didn't exchange a single word. The force of human compassion had thrown their worlds, normally light years apart, so far out of their regular orbits they nearly collided; but the more powerful force of mistrust and superficial habits had intervened to correct them from their momentary deviation.

As the two women got off the tram at the top of the hill, the wind whistled in their ears, swirling around them from head to toe, rustling through the dry leaves like a snake. They walked up a driveway to the tall white wall surrounding the hospital grounds, passed through a narrow pedestrian gate with a decorative iron grille, and found themselves in a quiet, sheltered world where even autumn walked on tiptoe. The trees here had more leaves than the ones on the street outside, and the roundly trimmed bushes were still as lushly green as in summer. The sky cleared for a moment, the clouds breaking up and swarming like iridescent amoebas under a microscope.

They walked up a path through manicured lawns, and as they reached the cardiology pavilion, the manager turned to Marie. "Just so you know, Mrs.

Kouřimská specifically requested that you come. The doctor said she asked for you several times. She said she needed to speak to you as soon as possible."

Marie, clutching the flowers to her chest to shield them from the wind, pulled up in amazement. "I thought it was strange that you asked me of all people to come along. I hardly even knew her. What do we have in common, huh? What could she want from me?"

Marie lifted her head and, probably for the first time in her life, looked into the manager's eyes from up close. As a ray of sun shone through the gap between the wisps of cloud, Marie noticed tiny gold dots sprinkled across the older woman's gray-green irises. The curtain opened for an instant, then fell back into place.

"I guess now you'll find out," the manager said. She strode off down a side path that led to the building's rear wing and a door with a black sign marked VISITORS.

They entered a small elongated lobby. A petite blonde in a white smock sat behind the desk talking on the phone. A stocky, dark-skinned man in a belted trench coat lifted himself from the bench along the wall and offered an awkward bow. An overstuffed black briefcase, almost as big as a suitcase, lay next to him on the bench.

The cinema manager nodded to him and with raised eyebrows turned to the receptionist, who was just finishing her conversation. She hung up the phone and looked at a list on the desk in front of her.

"You've come to see the lady in room sixty-eight, correct? Mrs. . . ." She slid her finger down the page. "Kouřimská, yes. The lieutenant is also here to see her. She asked me to have him come at the same time as you. The nurse will be here shortly." She pulled a file out of a drawer and began flipping through it.

The manager turned, walked to the window, and looked out at the garden. Marie studied the crumpled green paper wrapped around the bouquet. Vendyš stood next to the bench wearing the same hardened look he always did when he was uneasy.

The door opened and a big, beefy nurse walked in. Her puny cap sat perched atop her cropped gray hair like a white baby bird.

"Follow me," she said and set off down a long white corridor that twisted and turned so many times Marie lost her sense of direction. *If we go all the way to the end*, she thought, *I'll never be able to find my way back.* The hulking nurse strode along at such a brisk pace it was almost impossible to keep up. *We're trotting like horses*, Marie thought, panting and sweating in her overcoat. But just then they came to a door at the end of the corridor, and the nurse's mighty posterior blocked all further progress.

She motioned for them to wait and went inside. A moment later she came back out, closing the door behind her. "She wants to talk to the manager first. That's you, right?" She looked at the manager, then turned to Vendyš and Marie. "The two of you can go in after her. There are only two chairs in there anyway. Don't stay any longer than you need to, and ring for me if she needs anything." The nurse marched off at a racer's clip.

The manager took the bouquet from Marie. "I'll give her the flowers and pass along the girls' greetings. I don't want to tire her out, so I won't be long. Then I'll head back to work but, Marie, you stay here with her as long as you need to. No rush." She turned and stepped through the door.

Inside, it looked like the machine room of a small but highly efficient factory: instruments, flasks, and dials hanging all over the walls, resting on tables and stands, busily ticking and blinking. A pale, glowing dot bounced intermittently across a black screen over the bed, trailing a tail behind it like a tiny sprightly comet.

The woman's body on the bed was wrapped in wires and transparent tubing. A thin tendril led from the needle sticking out of her left wrist to a glass bottle, which every now and then gave off a deep gurgling sound. The skin around her cheekbones had sunken into a lunar landscape of tortuous valleys and gorges, her eyes plunged into shadow. The center of her silvery-white face was covered with a small oxygen mask like a muzzle.

The woman didn't move or open her eyes.

"Mrs. Kouřimská," the manager said quietly, laying the flowers on the bedside table.

A flicker of light appeared in the shadows. A white hand lifted up and removed the mask. The mouth, now exposed, smiled.

"Mrs. Kouřimská," the manager said once more, even softer. "How are you?"

"I died, did you know that? Then I rose from the dead like Jesus Christ," the woman in bed whispered. "You might not believe it, but it wasn't so terrible, really. The end . . . of everything. Good *and* bad. It was a relief. Life is overrated . . ."

"Mrs. Kouřimská," the manager said anxiously, "you mustn't lose hope."

"Hope? What for? It's just an eternity of waiting . . . for something that will never come. Do you have hope?"

The manager, visibly flustered, gave no reply.

"You see?" Mrs. Kouřimská said. "What good is hope to someone who's happy? It's only for the desperate. And once you stop despairing, you don't need hope anymore . . . just peace of mind . . . and even without hope, I believe that will come in the end."

Mrs. Kouřimská closed her eyes and placed the oxygen mask back on her mouth.

The manager looked around the room and spotted a glass vase on the shelf above the sink. She placed it in the sink and filled it with water. She took the bouquet of carnations from the nightstand, removed the paper, and arranged the long straight stems with the huge pink blossoms in the vase.

Suddenly she realized she'd made a mistake. *I should have brought her some ferns in a flowerpot*, she thought. The flowers' beauty interrupted the impersonal feel of the room, so perfectly designed for a person to quietly finish her life and return it like a book she had read to the end. The manager had to choke back her tears at the cruel and fragile preciousness of life.

She took the vase and placed it on a nightstand in the back by the wall, where the woman couldn't see it. Then she sat down on a chair and just quietly watched for a while.

"The girls send their best regards," she said finally. "We all miss you. Do you need anything?"

The woman in bed shook her head.

"Marie is here with me. And also Lieutenant Vendyš. I should probably go now, so you won't get too tired. If you want anything, just tell the nurse to let me know. She can even call me at home . . . any time." She paused a moment, then timidly reached out and touched the woman's white hand. "I can come again, if you want," she said.

Kouřimská just looked at her.

"Bye for now," the manager said, rising to her feet.

She stood by the bed a while, then suddenly sat back down. "One more thing, Mrs. Kouřimská. You may have wondered why nobody asked where you were that Friday afternoon and how come you didn't get into work until almost eight. Well, when the commotion broke out and the police showed up, I quickly checked the sign-in sheet and saw you weren't there. So I put you down as though you'd come in like you normally do, at two thirty. It never even occurred to the police that you weren't there that afternoon. And since they didn't know, they didn't ask anyone about it, and since they didn't ask, no one told them. You know the girls: they don't say anything they don't have to, and by some miracle Božena didn't notice. So, that's what I wanted to tell you, just in case you were wondering."

Mrs. Kouřimská stared at her in silence. Then she removed the hideous mask from her mouth again. "Thank you. I didn't deserve it, but thank you very much all the same." She closed her eyes again. "Why did you do it?"

"To keep things neat," the manager said drily. "I wanted them to go away and leave us alone. I knew you had nothing to do with the murder, and I wanted to save all of us the complications and headaches. If anyone had let something slip or the police had found out from Božena, I always could have said I put you down by mistake. I didn't lie to anyone, because nobody asked. So what could they do to me?"

"Thank you," Mrs. Kouřimská said again in a barely audible voice. "You're an incredible woman."

The manager stood up again. She touched the motionless hand on the blanket once more, then turned to leave.

"Mrs. Kouřimská," she said with her hand on the doorknob. "Just hold on."

"To what?" said the woman in bed. She almost smiled.

Lieutenant Vendyš sat at the head of the bed, tape recorder on his knees, holding a microphone to Mrs. Kouřimská's mouth. He didn't move a muscle once she began to speak. After a while his face went numb, which made him look almost brain-damaged. He tried hard not to think, not to judge, just to listen coolly and carefully. But the longer she talked, the more difficult it was.

Marie sat huddled in a chair beside the bed, not even daring to breathe. She could almost feel Mrs. Kouřimská's effort and fatigue in her own muscles and nerves; the desperate determination to tell it all while there was still time. Every sentence was punctuated with lengthy pauses, every few words, but what she said was clear.

It was obvious she had thought through every aspect of her story in detail, crossing out every unnecessary word, as though she knew, down to the last minute, how much time she had left and how much she could squeeze into it. Marie could see only one thing mattered to Mrs. Kouřimská now: testifying to what she knew and what she wanted. It was the last thing she would do in her life, and the most important. This moment represented the culmination of her entire existence.

". . . so now you know why Karel Novák died," Mrs. Kouřimská was saying. She breathed in and out laboriously several times. "I had to tell you. So that now, when I die, Hrůza won't be the only one who knows."

Kouřimská put her oxygen mask over her mouth and closed her eyes. After resting a while, she spoke again, her voice clear and calm.

"It wasn't till Nedoma told me that that it dawned on me what I was doing. Up until then, I'd always thought I was just supplying him with gossip—ordinary stupid stuff that couldn't hurt anyone . . . and I needed the money," she added with some insistence.

It was quiet again for a while, the only sound the chatter and ticking of the instruments around them.

"But then it hit me: A man had lost his life and I was responsible . . . I helped drive him to suicide. I realized there's no such thing as a 'little' bad thing, because nobody can predict what will come of it . . . it can grow into a big thing, before you even know it . . ."

Marie leaned forward in her chair, feeling an urge to caress her hand, say something soothing. But Mrs. Kouřimská stared up at the ceiling, doggedly pushing ahead:

"No one can do a thing to stop people like Hrůza . . . They're like earthquakes, or the plague. But they could never inflict so much misery if it weren't for little bastards like Nedoma . . . the little helpers who try to convince you it doesn't matter, there's nothing wrong with a little snitching . . . They make evil seem like a natural, trivial thing . . . They blur the line between guilt and innocence, till eventually you accept it and murder just seems like an accident with nobody to blame . . . That's why I killed him."

Vendyš squeezed his fingers so hard the microphone almost popped out of his hand. The blood drained from Marie's face and tiny drops of sweat broke out on her upper lip. The woman in bed paused briefly, then went on, her breathing labored but her voice calm and deliberate.

"After Nedoma told me Novák was dead, I didn't hear from him for a couple of weeks. Then that Friday morning he called and told me not to go to work . . . said he'd stop by for me later. He came over . . . and told me we had to keep going, we couldn't just give up because of a single mishap . . . by which he meant Novák's death . . . He said the job wasn't finished . . . in fact he was getting it up and running again . . . He said he'd also called you, Marie . . . said he'd decided to bring you on board and was going to meet you on Steep Street at eight . . . Hrůza would straighten Helena out, I'd get new instructions . . ."

Mrs. Kouřimská put the oxygen mask on her mouth and closed her eyes. The dot of light on-screen fluttered like a panicked butterfly, before settling back down again, bounding up and down along its crooked path. *Hang on*, Marie begged the dot in her mind. *Just hang on long enough for her to finish!*

Mrs. Kouřimská continued again in her calm, emotionless voice: "I said fine . . . He always drank beer when he came over . . . I dropped a pill in his glass in the kitchen, one of those ones the doctor prescribed to help me sleep . . . I put a sharp new knife in my handbag . . . asked if he could give me a lift to work, since he was heading there anyway . . . It was getting late . . . He started nodding off at the wheel on the way over . . . For a while I hoped we would just crash and the whole thing would be over . . . for both of us . . . but we made it . . . As soon as he stopped the car he fell asleep. I just sat there a while, feeling faint . . . The street was deserted . . . I took out the knife . . . looked around . . . not a soul . . . Suddenly it all became clear . . . I used to work in a hospital . . . I knew what to do . . ."

The woman lay still again, breathing in and out through her oxygen mask. The dot on-screen slowed to a limp. The instruments hummed and bubbled like an artificial stream.

"I didn't panic till afterwards . . . I jumped out of the car and ran in the other direction . . . that's where I got lucky . . . I had to walk all the way around the block to get into the Horizon . . . but at least I didn't have to go past the snack bar . . . so Božena couldn't see me through that glass wall of hers . . . and she didn't spot me when I came in the lobby, either. It was too crowded . . .

"Then at the top of the stairs I got an idea . . . I turned and went back to the snack bar . . . and told Božena to give me a pack of cigarettes, quick, I'd just finished mine . . . of course she assumed I just popped up from downstairs . . . I never dreamed I'd get away with it . . . If anyone had mentioned I wasn't at work that afternoon . . . but nobody said a thing . . . it was a miracle . . ."

She barely gasped out the last few words, then took a long break. When she finally started up again, Marie had to lean in close to make out what she was saying.

"I had blood on my gloves. I remembered I'd found a handbag in the auditorium recently that somebody had left there with a pair of scissors inside . . . I'd put it in the manager's office for safekeeping . . . I waited for her to step out, found the bag, took the scissors . . . I cut up the gloves and flushed them down the toilet . . . but meanwhile the manager went home and locked the office . . . I couldn't put the scissors back, so I wiped them off and stuck them behind the mirror in the ladies' room . . . I didn't want to get caught with them on me . . ."

She was wheezing now. Marie felt like telling her, *Enough, you've said enough already*, but couldn't bring herself to utter a word. Mrs. Kouřimská lay perfectly still, eyes closed, mask over her mouth. At length she started up again.

"Nobody suspected me . . . except for Hrůza . . . I don't know if he saw me, or whether he figured it out . . . but he knew, and he knew I was dangerous and had to get rid of me . . ."

She paused a moment, then added, "It must have

been a shock for Marie here when she came and saw what happened."

Marie got up, walked to the faucet, and poured herself a glass of water. She took a deep drink, then managed to rasp, "I saw it as soon as I got to the car. The knife, the blood . . . First I was terrified, then I thought I'd better come up with an alibi, quick. So I ran over to the pub. They know me there, so I hoped maybe that would get me out of it."

There was another moment of silence, then Mrs. Kouřimská said, "That's all I have to tell you, Lieutenant . . . That's everything . . . Now, if you don't mind . . . I'd like a moment . . . with Marie . . ."

Vendyš started as if waking from a trance. He pressed the stop button on the tape recorder, then just sat staring blankly at the ground. Mrs. Kouřimská didn't stir, but Marie said impatiently, "Did you hear what she said, Mr. Vendyš? We'd like a moment alone. It is her right, isn't it? So please go now." She gestured with her head toward the bed.

Vendyš stood up and shoved the tape recorder into his black briefcase, which was lying on the floor next to his chair. "Miss Vránová, stop by my office around six. I'll need you to sign the protocol." He hesitated a moment, taking in the ghostly face on the pillow.

"Good-bye, Mrs. Kouřimská," he said softly, then turned and left the room.

Marie got up, opened the door, and looked down the corridor. She walked back over to the bed and tried to smile. "You know I had no idea you were spying on us. I never would've guessed."

Mrs. Kouřimská opened her eyes but didn't look at Marie. She was probably too weak to turn her head. She stared up at the ceiling, breathing wheezily. Then her white hand stirred again and the tired butterfly fluttered.

"Marie," she said almost too softly to hear, breathing deeply in and out. "I knew . . . from the very start . . . about you . . . and the fat man . . . with the glasses . . . But I didn't tell . . . Nedoma . . . I would never . . . have done that . . ."

Marie's eyes widened and her mouth went dry again.

"Nothing got past me," Mrs. Kouřimská wheezed. "You wouldn't believe . . . I guess I had a born talent for snooping . . ." The shadows suddenly lifted from the corners of her mouth, which almost made it look like she was smiling.

As the white hand lifted, the butterfly skipped and pranced, but the hand failed to reach the face, sinking back onto the covers in exhaustion. The woman in bed coughed weakly. Marie glanced up at the monitor but the butterfly had disappeared and in its place a straight line of light extended across the black screen.

6

THE DAY OF the funeral was like a leap back in time to Indian summer. The cemetery paths had dried in the sun and the late-blooming asters had opened their blossoms on the graves. The last brown leaves sprinkled onto the lawn, which was still thick and green. The rich fall colors blended tastefully, just the way Mrs. Kouřimská used to like it, giving the cemetery a warm, cozy feel. *It's peaceful here*, the manager thought. *It has everything she needs.*

The funeral was at noon, so everyone on the Horizon staff turned out for it, including the box office girl, the accountant, and the cleaning ladies.

Even the projectionist showed up, a quiet bald little man of unassuming appearance, whose existence almost no one except the manager was aware of. He kept his distance from the others, restlessly shuffling his feet and staring at the ground. The women stood in a circle around the coffin, which was adorned with three huge bronze-colored chrysanthemums, thinking of the deceased, or rather the idea of her they had formed during her lifetime. Each of them was so different from the others that if anyone had been able to see into their thoughts, they never would have guessed that they represented the same person. As is true for all of us, Mrs. Kouřimská's innermost self was cut into a thousand facets, and everyone who knew her found at least one of them that reflected what they were looking for, based on their own personalities.

There was a sharp smell of damp earth as the priest's voice scattered in the autumn acoustics. The ceremony was nearly over when there was a crackling of dry leaves and a pudgy young girl in grubby jeans and torn sneakers shuffled up to the grave. She had straight hair cut short and round red cheeks, and she worked a piece of chewing gum in her mouth. She came to a stop at the edge of the grave and propped her hands on her hips, slouching slightly at the waist. Chewing intently, she stared down into the open grave with such a peculiar look on her face that some of the women were afraid she was going to spit her gum onto the coffin. But the girl just stood there a moment or two, then turned and waded away through the brown layer of leaves.

Ládinka wiped away her tears and leaned over to Líba. "Please, where does a girl like that get off showin' her face here! Mrs. Kouřimská was a lady."

"You think?" Líba said softly, watching the girl's wide, swaying hips disappear down the path through the graves.

They slowly made their way toward the cemetery exit in the slightly exhilarated mood typical of people who have just buried someone they aren't too close to. Maybe it was the atmosphere of the cemetery, the one peaceful place in a big city. Maybe it was the relief of having such a depressing experience behind them. Maybe being so close to death intensified the feeling of being alive. Who knows? But whatever the case, all the participants in Mrs. Kouřimská's funeral, including the tearful Ládinka, had to consciously restrain themselves from talking too loudly and work to maintain a suitable level of decorum.

Even Helena loosened up a little. She attached herself

to Marie, and at one point, when Marie bent down to pick up some red and yellow maple leaves, Helena stopped alongside her a few steps behind the others, so Marie decided to take advantage of the opportunity. "So, Helena, don't you think it's time you started lookin' for another job? I mean, Líba's leavin' in a couple days and Ládinka won't last long without her. She already said she's goin' to see if she can find a better spot. I'm probably takin' off too. I don't like the looks of that new gal they sent to replace Kouřimská. She's gonna suck our blood dry, mark my words. Anyways, I'm sick of the whole cinema and workin' nights all the time. Soon as something turns up, I quit. What about you? You can't stay there forever. What did you ever get out of that job except trouble, huh? Tell me that."

Helena bowed her head. "You're right, Marie. The place is like a toxic dump, and without you there it'll be even worse. But I can't. I don't care where I am or what I do. I know you don't understand, but I don't want anything else. Nothing's going to change for me, no matter what happens."

Marie nodded. "You might be surprised, but I think I understand. It's like fallin' off a moving train. Suddenly everything's just flyin' by and there's no way to get back on. But give it some time. It'll change. Always does. And there's always another train coming."

"I know. It's just I don't think I could even get on if it stopped right in front of me."

They reached the cemetery gate, where everyone else was waiting for them. Nobody felt like going back to the noise and stress of the outside world. The manager looked at her watch. "Well, it can't be helped, we have to go," she said apologetically. "It's that time."

All thoughts of Mrs. Kouřimská vanished from their minds.

"That was nice," Ládinka said as the ushers descended the stairs back at the Horizon. "I didn't expect to have such a good time."

By nighttime the temperature had plummeted. Helena shivered walking home in her thin coat. It wasn't that much warmer in her studio than on the street.

She lit the gas in the oven and collapsed, fully dressed, onto the couch. The flat warmed up pretty quickly, but Helena just lay there, staring up at the ceiling. *I can't*, she said in her head, then in a whisper, and finally out loud. *I can't, I can't do it anymore. If only I had a child at least. Anything at all. I can't. I can't, I can't get up every morning and struggle my way through the day just to fall into bed like a zombie at night and get up and do it all over again in the morning. I can't and I don't want to. What happened to me? What happened to Karel? Tell me, Karel, what awful thing happened to make you forget about me? Why, Karel? For God's sake, how could you abandon me? If only you had at least left me some kind of message, a word, a sentence . . . I can't, I can't go on living in this incomprehensible world.*

All of a sudden the heat in her flat became unbearable. She tried to get up from the couch, but her legs gave way beneath her, as if even her own weight was too much to bear. *I've got a stone in my heart. Forever. As long as I live.*

She dragged herself to the stove and turned off the gas. Leaning against the hot metal with both her hands, she stood a while thinking. Then she turned the gas on again, but didn't light it. She took off her coat and lay back down on the couch. She closed her eyes, listening to the soft hiss of the gas. Her head began to spin. *Just this one thing and after that, I'll never have to do anything . . . ever again . . .*

The telephone rang. Helena didn't move. It kept ringing. There was no reason for anything, there was no point. It didn't matter if she picked up the phone or not. It wouldn't change a thing. Nothing could. The phone rang again. She reached out and lifted the receiver.

"Helena, it's me, Vojta," said the soft voice on the other end. "Listen, I know how you feel . . . It's torturing me . . . I tried, you know that . . . Helena, do you hear me? Can I ever see you again? Just as friends?"

Helena laid the phone down on the table. *Vojta . . . Karel's shadow . . . I wish he had disappeared along with him . . . Karel's envoy . . .* She took a deep breath.

A spark went off in her darkened brain: *Karel's envoy . . . what if he really is Karel's envoy, what if Karel . . . what if it means that Karel doesn't want me to . . .*

She slid off the couch onto the floor and crawled on all fours to the window. With one hand she gripped the windowsill while with the other she reached for the handle. She flung the window open wide and curled up on the floor underneath it, shaking with cold and exhaustion, as the air from outside swept through the room. Finally, after a long time, she stood, walked unsteadily to the stove, and shut off the gas. She put her coat back on and laid the phone in the cradle. She stretched out on the couch for a while again, no longer shaking, despite the bitter cold. Finally she got up, walked to the window, and stared out into the black sky.

The humidity had risen slightly and the temperature had dropped. As tiny drops of moisture condensed in the air, a splendidly shaped, perfectly symmetrical star split off from a low-hanging cloud, the first snowflake of the year, drifting slowly down through the night. Helena reached her hand out the window and caught the chilly flake in her palm. Instantly it began to melt. Helena gasped. "Karel," she said out loud. "Karel, are you with me? Are you the stone in my heart? Stay! Stay with me and I'll gladly bear it. I can. I must."

She closed the window and lay back down on the couch. Slowly the room began to warm up. The telephone started to ring again, but this time Helena didn't pick up.

I'm not going to talk to him now . . . I don't care if he understands . . . I'm not letting anyone else's voice in here now . . . Maybe later, sometime . . . a long time from now . . .

She fell asleep in her clothes on the couch, with one hand under her head. All night long, drops slid from the pools in her eyes onto the coarse cloth of the upholstery, but gradually the deep lines around her mouth faded.

The snow outside the window thickened, lofting up with the wind, the flakes dancing and swirling in all their sparkling glory, until finally they fell to the ground and transformed into mud.

But every now and then one of them got caught on a tree branch or in a crack between the centuries-old tiles of the Malá Strana rooftops, so even though the snowfall lasted just a while, some glittering touches of white remained tucked away till morning, when the people began to emerge from their homes into the new day, into the same old aimless wandering.

7

⁓

IT WAS A small square room, the walls painted dirty gray floor to ceiling, with a stack of filing cabinets along one of them painted a gray two shades darker. A desk, bare except for an open folder of documents, a rack holding a row of pipes, and a battered ashtray. On the wall facing it, the plain black rectangle of a window reflected the room's interior like a blind mirror. There was nothing else in the room except two comfortable chairs with two men seated in them: one fat, the other even fatter.

The fat man with glasses sat on the chair for visitors, by the window, trying to sound rational and coherent.

But in the pressure cooker of the overheated, smoke-filled room, his fatigue ran rampant, his head buzzing and colors flickering before his eyes. He yawned till his ears popped. That helped wake him up a little.

The hard lines of exhaustion seemed out of place on his plump-cheeked face, inclined by nature to a kindhearted smile. He looked like Mr. Pickwick being stretched on the rack as the fatter man silently fixed him with a stare.

"Listen," the fat man said at last. "I already told you the gist of it. The rest can wait till tomorrow, can't it? I've hardly slept in three nights and I'm not thinking too straight . . ."

He took off his glasses and rubbed his eyes.

"I hope you realize," the fatter man said officiously, laying his pipe in the ashtray for emphasis, "that you came back almost one month late, in gross violation . . . So, back to the murder on Steep Street!"

"All right, fine, fine," the fat man said with a sigh. "I'll do my best. But be patient with me."

He slumped another bit lower in his chair and stretched out his legs in front of him. Then he took off his glasses and swung them in his fingers, eyes fixed to the ceiling.

"Well, despite our assumptions, Kouřimská wasn't a nice lady at all," he began slowly. "She was actually a strange and pretty frightening person, when you get right down to it. Not like Nedoma—she wasn't a murderer or a sadist—but she needed a lot of cash, and she had no way to get it, so she signed on as an informant." He gave another sigh. "As noted earlier, this isn't particularly uncommon for us, and Kouřimská followed a fairly established recipe. She figured she'd outsmart us. Supply us with some trivial information, do us some harmless favors, keep the wolf well-fed . . . and she got away with it for a pretty long time. Nedoma would plant her in some inconspicuous spot and she'd tell him who was talking to who, who they were talking about, who was in bed with who—the usual gossip. I guess she got used to it. It was a lucrative sideline. Didn't do any serious harm. She never said a word to Nedoma about me and Marie, for instance. Maybe what she was doing wasn't that good, but she was convinced it wasn't that bad, either. And that's where the hitch comes in." The fat man sat up straight in his chair, put on his glasses, and narrowed his eyes at the fatter man.

"Where?" the fatter man asked through a cloud of smoke.

"Most people can't imagine something unless they've had the experience themselves. That's why half the time they don't realize what they're doing. Kouřimská helped Nedoma and Hrůza set an ambush for Helena Nováková not out of ill will, but because she literally couldn't imagine how much Novák's wife meant to him. She was incapable of the kind of relationship they had, so it never even crossed her mind that something like that could exist. For her it was just an assignment like any other—only this time it ended in death. The death of Karel Novák. And everyone is affected by death. People understand death based on future experience, so to speak, the only one that no one on this earth can avoid, and this was not only death, but a violent, premature death—a murder in fact. Any attempt at innocent games can't help but end in murder. Novák's death came as a huge shock to Kouřimská. Suddenly she was horrified."

The fat man cleared his throat and again took off his glasses. The moment he stopped speaking, his whole body relaxed, beginning to slip into sleep like a bath of warm water. He rubbed his eyes and shook himself like a dog.

"And to top it all off, Kouřimská was a religious woman. When she had the stroke and realized how little time she had left, she was desperate to repent. She probably thought if she took the blame for Nedoma's death to save Maric, it would atone for the part she played in Novák's death and redeem her sins. She knew no one here on earth could hurt her anymore. But she wanted to set her reputation right with the big man up top. I can just imagine her lying there in the hospital, churning it all over in her head, getting her story straight, polishing and refining it, checking it for holes . . ."

The fatter man pulled the ashtray toward him and knocked out his pipe. "I'm sure this is all an accurate analysis of Mrs. Kouřimská's mental state, but it doesn't particularly interest me. I'm a simple man. I just want an objective account of the facts. If you'd be so kind," he said with an edge in his voice.

The fat man slumped down in his chair to a near-horizontal position.

"It was like a merry-go-round," he went on, sounding half-asleep. "Vendyš suspected Hrůza, but he was too high up for Vendyš to get to. Besides which, Hrůza had to keep him at arm's length as long as there was a risk that Kouřimská might talk. He had to get rid of her as quickly and discreetly as possible—she knew too much. Kouřimská was scared to death of him, but when it came to Nedoma's murder, she suspected Marie."

He thought a moment, then added, "I'd really like to know what's going to happen now that Kouřimská has let on why Novák killed himself. Vendyš took the whole thing down in a detailed statement that Marie signed as a witness that same evening. Well, given that Kouřimská and Nedoma are dead now and can't testify, and Marie's in so deep she won't breathe a word, they'll probably hush the whole thing up and smooth it over as usual," the fat man said philosophically.

"Please," said the fatter man, clearly losing his patience, "just take it from the beginning. I realize it's all swirling around inside your head, but this is a complex case and I need it to be clear. Start from the Friday when Nedoma called up Vránová."

"Okay, right, that's how it started." The fat man yawned again, leaned his arms on the armrests, and slowly raised himself to a sitting position.

"I could use a cup of coffee, if you don't mind," he said. "But none of that dishwater slop. Something that packs a punch."

The fatter man shot him an unfriendly look, but opened the bottom drawer of his desk and pulled out a little red electric coffeepot. He shook it to make sure there was water inside, then turned to insert the plug into the socket in the wall behind his chair. Reaching back into the drawer, he fished out a battered earthenware mug, a teaspoon, and a loud yellow can, loaded two heaping teaspoons of coffee into the mug, and splashed water over it from the pot, which had meanwhile begun to bubble. Digging around again, he unearthed two grimy sugar cubes and pushed them across the desk along with the mug and the spoon.

The fat man took the mug in both hands, stared into it in disgust, and took a sip.

"So that Friday afternoon," he began in a slight singsong as though telling a fairy tale, "Nedoma called Marie Vránová at the Horizon and told her he needed to meet her that night at eight. Right away, from the tone of his voice, Marie could tell it was bad. She's an extremely clever woman, in her own way, whereas Nedoma was a downright moron, and a dirtbag to boot. Marie had him pegged from the start. Which is why she was so scared. You see, I myself was supposed to come in that afternoon for a handoff, less than a half hour later. So Marie's got this huge bandage on her behind, and she knows Nedoma, sneaky bastard that he is, might have called just to make sure she was there, and could have her arrested at any moment. Of course she had no idea how much he actually knew, but she guessed that he only suspected her, since if he'd had any proof he would have locked her up right on the spot. It wasn't a lost cause yet, but she needed to take action, fast. At first she was so frightened, though, she didn't know which way to turn."

The fat man finished his coffee and set the empty mug on the desk. "Then there's this," he said. "The day before, Marie had found a pair of scissors somebody dropped under one of the seats and she just picked them up without thinking. So now she reaches into the pocket of her uniform and they slip right into her hand. All of a sudden a light bulb goes off in her head. She goes running into the ladies' room, peels off the bandage, cuts it up, and flushes it down the toilet—except when it comes to the middle piece with the microdots, she can't do it. I tell you, that Marie's got some guts," the fat man said. "Talk about a gamble!"

He watched with a faraway look as the fatter man scraped out his pipe.

"We had a kind of a primitive warning signal agreed—you know, the usual: newspaper cutouts—for a situation like this, in case something went wrong. So Marie used the scissors to snip up an old *Rudé právo* and by some miracle I managed to decipher that her cover had been blown and I needed to be on the street around the corner at eight o'clock. She barely finished it in time for me to come rolling in, and of course instead of an envelope with a bandage in it I stick my hand in my pocket and come out with a fistful of newspaper. Needless to say, I got bored with the movie pretty quick, so I shuffled out of there and got lost."

The fatter man put down his pipe, folded his arms, and tilted his head as though finally he was starting to get interested.

"Like I said, it took some divine assistance to work out what Marie's message said. But the other thing I fished out of my pocket was a squished chocolate truffle. And when I cut it open, there were six tiny pieces of bandage inside, with a microdot on each one. She did such a clever job of folding them up, they weren't even damaged. I mean, can you believe it? She figured that, no matter what happened, I could always swallow the truffle or step on it, so she took the risk. That is one cunning vixen, I tell you," the fat man said, starry-eyed. He reveled in the thought a moment before going on.

"Oh, I almost forgot. Marie wiped off the scissors and stuck them behind the mirror in the ladies' room. She wanted to make sure she was clean as a whistle, get rid of anything that suggested any connection to me or, even more important, those cutouts I had in my pocket. The interesting thing is, Vendyš somehow sensed the scissors had something to do with Nedoma's case. He kept trying to find the link, and Kouřimská also ingeniously managed to work them into her fairy tale. She probably thought we'd found a trace of blood on them so she had to explain."

The fat man didn't look even a little jolly anymore. The closer he got to the climax of his story, the more his face revealed, like a palimpsest, a graphic record of those awful minutes that Friday night.

"Well, I had plenty of time till eight to get organized and think it all through. I didn't even really need to. I took care of the microdots and a couple other things, as per instructions . . ."—he glanced up at the fatter man but got no reaction—". . . so shortly before eight o'clock I took up my position on Steep Street. I still didn't really know what I was waiting for, or what I was going to do when it happened. It looked like a plague had hit, the place was so dead, but not for long. Next thing I knew, Nedoma's car pulled up to the sidewalk and a minute later Kouřimská jumped out and shot off like a bullet. Not up toward the entrance to the Horizon on Broad, but the other way, down Steep Street—probably so no one could spot her from the snack bar on the corner. I casually strolled past the car, peeked in, and saw Nedoma in there snoring away, out for the count. So I ducked into the doorway of the nearest building, switched off the safety on the gun in my pocket, and poked out my nose to make sure the coast was clear, when all of a sudden I see a thin man in a beige suit turn into Steep Street. Striding along quick and easy, like a soldier. When he got to Nedoma's car he stopped and leaned in the window on the passenger side for a couple seconds, where Kouřimská was sitting before. Then he straightened back up and marched off down Steep Street again, just as quick and calm as he'd come. As soon as he was around the corner, I went to take a look and saw that he'd saved me the trouble."

The fat man hunched over in his chair and thought a moment.

"Steep Street is practically made for a knife," he said. His voice was slow with sleepiness and husky, perhaps with the memory of the darkness on Steep Street. He laid a palm on his eyes and rubbed them as if trying to erase the sight from his mind.

"I know, pal," the fatter man said. All of a sudden his voice changed, as if he were up on stage addressing an audience, some unseen third person in the room. "I know how you feel. It isn't a pleasant experience. I wish the world were different, too. I wish we could all live in peace and none of this was necessary. But, sadly enough . . ."

He was too simple to grasp the look directed at him through the rounded lenses of the fat man's glasses. His

voice trailed off and he went back to scraping his pipe.
The fat man drew in a deep breath.

"The worst was yet to come. Because then I turn
around and see Marie sashaying past the snack bar
onto Steep Street. Almost gave me a heart attack.
Naturally I figured she'd stay holed up in the
Horizon, where everyone could see her, so whatever
else happened she'd have a rock-solid alibi. And here
she was, traipsing around like Little Bo Peep, the
nosy minx," the fat man said affectionately, cheering
up a bit.

"Not to mention it's a gross violation . . ." the fatter
man interjected.

"Oh yeah. But you can't look at it that way with her.
I waved to her to get lost and you should've seen how
she tore out of there! Apart from that, you've got to
admit she handled it with flying colors—even without
instructions," the fat man said acerbically, then sat a
while lost in thought.

"You know," he said at last. "I think it must've gone
something like this: Hrůza's ship was going down.
His methods aren't in fashion anymore and Nedoma
had enough on him to make a mess of his lovely, carefully cultivated career. The times call for subtlety, for
players who can twist and dodge, and Nedoma isn't
capable of that kind of finesse. So Hrůza made up

his mind to get rid of him, and he was just waiting for the perfect opportunity. Nedoma gave it to him when he walked in to report that he had a strong suspicion about Marie, but dammit, he didn't have proof. My guess is they put their heads together and Hrůza came up with an idea. He ordered Nedoma to bring in Kouřimská to help put the screws on Marie—how, we'll never find out now, but effectively enough to make her come clean. So Nedoma, obedient as ever, carried out the order, which in turn gave Hrůza the ideal opportunity to do him in such a way that suspicion would have to fall on Marie, or, if he really got lucky, Kouřimská."

"In that case, he seriously miscalculated . . ."

"Oh, God yes. Even for people like Hrůza, not everything in the world works out the way they planned. But anyway, imagine the pleasant surprise he got when he stuck his head in the window and saw Nedoma fast asleep. Everything went smooth as silk. Of course Kouřimská still took some work, but she made it a lot easier on him by dropping dead before he could even lay a hand on her. So in the end everything turned out alright, and Vojtěch Hrůza is safe and sound and will live happily ever after."

"Now, now," the fatter man said, reverting to his artificial voice. "You need to take it easy and get yourself some sleep. After that, things will look different." He fixed the fat man with a look of electric intensity produced by total concentration and the suppression of any distracting influences; in fact you could say it was a direct result of his simplicity. He immediately recognized that the fat man's fatigue wouldn't disappear no matter how much rest he got. He might never get over it.

"What do you mean?" he asked. "What really happened between Nedoma and Kouřimská?"

"Well, the way me and Marie figured it . . ."

"Wait a minute. When did this figuring take place? You realize personal contact is to be restricted to extreme—"

"This is an extreme situation," the fat man exploded. "How else was I supposed to find out what story Kouřimská told them at the hospital? How else was I supposed to assess whether Marie was out of danger and I could get the hell out? You may not realize," he snapped, "but this was top priority for me, an extreme case, as you would say. We got together the night after Kouřimská's death, and we both agreed it must've been something like this: After Novák's death, Kouřimská swore she'd never have anything to with Nedoma again. If he wasn't such an idiot, he would've seen for himself that she was a nervous wreck and couldn't be counted on anymore. But instead he went back to her that Friday—probably on Hrůza's orders—and told her the agent they had been after all that time wasn't Helena Nováková, but actually Marie. And they were going to expose her that night. I'm sure he said 'expose.' That's their favorite word," the fat man said in disgust. "Then he probably explained to her what she was supposed to do. But that was the one thing Kouřimská didn't want to do for anything in the world.

"I don't know how Nedoma sniffed us out, but we shouldn't have been surprised. Once he got over his fixation on Nováková, sooner or later he had to fall for Marie. We should have scrapped the whole thing as soon as that kid got murdered. It was exceedingly risky, once they locked up Fišer, that kid who was sleeping with Novák's secretary . . ."

"Risky, yes, but I wouldn't say exceedingly," the fatter man said coolly, taking another filthy pipe from the rack. "I can assure you, however, that the Horizon has screened its last show. And Vránová's acting days are over. I assume Hrůza will leave her alone now, in his own interest, but we won't be using her anymore. And you need to get some rest. After that we'll see . . ."

The fat man shot him another glare, which the fatter man ignored.

"So to finish what I was saying," the fat man said. "As far as I can tell, Kouřimská decided that she was going to warn Marie. She mixed the barbiturate into Nedoma's beer to gain time, but by the time she made it to the cinema, Marie was already gone. Kouřimská must have realized what a dangerous situation she'd gotten herself into, so she had to cover herself somehow. As a precaution, she went the long way, all the way around the block, which is why she missed Marie. And when she didn't run into her downstairs either, she ran back up to the snack bar to try and catch a glimpse of her on the street through the window, but by then it was too late. There was nothing anyone could do. When word got out that Nedoma had been murdered, Kouřimská must have concluded Marie was the one who did it."

"Sounds like a plausible explanation," the fatter man said, pulling some shreds of tobacco from a leather pouch and stuffing them into his pipe. "What was the lieutenant's reaction to her confession?"

"Marie got the impression he didn't buy it. Unlike Nedoma, Vendyš is no fool, and he probably figured out Kouřimská was covering for someone, but what could he do? Her statement fit with the facts as far as he knew, and she gave it on her deathbed in the presence of a witness. I reckon he had no choice but to close the case, but I'm sure it'll be haunting him for a while."

"I'm really at the end of my tether right now, but remind me to have a good laugh about all this someday," the fat man said bitterly. "The thing is, Vendyš might have been able to nail Hrůza down in the end. His instinct and experience had him heading the right direction the whole time. But Mrs. Kouřimská, who wanted to do a good deed before she died—save someone's life and earn her redemption—made it impossible. She saved a serial killer who ended up bringing about her death as well."

There was a moment of silence. The fat man took off his glasses, yawned, and slumped down in the chair, stretching his legs out in front of him. "Well, the main thing is, Marie's in the clear now, for good," he said with a thin smile.

"So if there really is somebody up there weighing our deeds, he's going to have one hell of a time with Mrs. Kouřimská," he sighed again, closing his eyes. "I just hope it isn't like here. Because if we got what we deserved for everything we did in our lives, they'd have to just cancel heaven, straight up."

"Amen," said the fatter man, packing tobacco into his pipe. He tucked it between his teeth and looked around for matches. As his eyes passed over the black rectangle of the window, he noticed some fleecy streaks of white stuck to it from outside.

"Look at that," said the fatter man almost humanly and struck a match. "The first snow!"

But the fat man was fast asleep.

NOTES

A few of the characters in *Innocence* have surnames with meanings relevant to their personalities or their role in the plot. They are listed here (in alphabetical order) along with explanations of references in the novel that are common knowledge to Czech readers but most non-Czechs are likely to miss.

Dolejš: lower

Hrůza: horror, terror, dread

Nedoma: not at home

Navrátil: Josef Matěj Navrátil, Czech painter (1798–1865). Famous for his landscapes, although most of his work consisted of still lifes and figurative paintings. He is also known for having inspired the work of photographer Josef Sudek.

State Security: in Czech, *Státní bezpečnost*, Communist Czechoslovakia's secret police (commonly referred to by its abbreviation, StB).

"good princess Libuše": Legend has it that Libuše was the wise and beautiful wife of the Czech ruler Přemysl. One day, as she stood overlooking the Vltava river from the fortress of Vyšehrad where she and Přemysl lived, she prophesied the creation of Prague with the words, "I see a great city whose glory will touch the stars." Seeing a man building the threshold of a house (in Czech, *práh*), she ordered a castle erected on the site and suggested the city be named *Praha*. In another legend, made famous by Alois Jirásek's *Staré pověsti české* (1894; *Old Czech Legends*), Šemík was the name of the crafty white horse that saved the farmer Horymír's life by leaping over the ramparts of Vyšehrad with him just before he was to be executed.

"what a nice statue they'd made of her": Božena Němcová (1820–62), author of the classic *Babička* (1855;
The Grandmother), one of the first novels written in
Czech. An idealized retelling of the author's childhood,
it is known and revered as a repository of folk wisdom.
Born Barbara Pankel in Vienna, Němcová wed at age
17, in an arranged and ultimately unhappy marriage.
She died, alone and in poverty, in Prague. She is currently pictured on the Czech 500-crown banknote.

ABOUT THE AUTHOR

Heda Margolius Kovály was born Heda Bloch in 1919 to Jewish parents in Prague. In 1941, her family was deported to the Łódź ghetto in Poland. Heda, her parents, and her husband, Rudolf Margolius, survived horrific conditions there, only to be taken to Auschwitz in 1944. On arrival Heda's parents perished in the gas chambers. She and Rudolf were separated, but Heda survived by being selected for work detail, and eventually escaped a death march in time to participate in the Prague Uprising. In Prague, she was reunited with Rudolf, who rose to deputy minister of foreign trade after the 1948 Communist takeover of Czechoslovakia.

In 1952, Rudolf was arrested on false charges of con-
spiring against the state and convicted in the Slánský
Trial, one of the most notorious Stalinist show trials of
the era. In the wake of her husband's execution, Heda,
who had been working as a graphic designer, and
her five-year-old son, Ivan, found themselves societal
outcasts. Denied employment and thrown out of her
apartment, Heda eked out a living by designing book
dust jackets and weaving carpets. In 1955, she married
Pavel Kovály, a philosophy lecturer. Heda turned to
translation, and eventually earned a reputation as one
of the country's leading literary translators. Following
the 1968 Soviet invasion of Czechoslovakia, Heda
and Pavel sought a new home in the United States,
where Pavel worked as a professor at Northeastern
University in Boston, and Heda was a librarian at Harvard Law School. They returned to Prague in 1996.
Heda died in 2010 at the age of 91. *Under a Cruel Star,*
her memoir of her time in concentration camps and
the early years of Czechoslovak communism, was first
published in 1973 and has since been translated into
many languages.

ABOUT THE TRANSLATOR

Alex Zucker has translated novels by Czech authors
Jáchym Topol, Miloslava Holubová, Petra Hůlová, and
Patrik Ouředník. Honors he has received include an
English PEN Award for Writing in Translation, an
NEA Literary Fellowship, and the ALTA National
Translation Award. In 2014 he created new subtitles
for the digitally restored version of *Closely Watched
Trains*, the 1966 Czechoslovak New Wave classic
based on the Bohumil Hrabal novella. Alex lives in
the Greenpoint neighborhood of Brooklyn, New
York. Visit him online at alexjzucker.com.